Oliver Thorne Miller

Four-handed Folk

Oliver Thorne Miller

Four-handed Folk

ISBN/EAN: 9783744769419

Printed in Europe, USA, Canada, Australia, Japan

Cover: Foto ©Andreas Hilbeck / pixelio.de

More available books at **www.hansebooks.com**

MR. CROWLEY

FOUR-HANDED FOLK

BY

OLIVE THORNE MILLER

WITH ILLUSTRATIONS

BOSTON AND NEW YORK
HOUGHTON, MIFFLIN AND COMPANY
The Riverside Press, Cambridge
1896

The Riverside Press, Cambridge, Mass., U. S. A.
Electrotyped and Printed by H. O. Houghton & Co.

CONTENTS.

LIST OF ILLUSTRATIONS.

FOUR-HANDED FOLK.

I.

THE KINKAJOU.

I. NIPSEY.

The way it came about that a bird-student set up a menagerie in her parlor, was this. In New York the shops that keep birds for sale are also supplied with beasts. In the largest of them one may buy almost anything, from a white mouse to an elephant, and always when I go there to look for birds, I pass into the room beyond and look at the animals. There is generally a cage or two of monkeys, and half a dozen or more of other animals, just imported from abroad, and not yet placed in some museum or zoölogical garden.

One day while I was going through the room, I stopped before a cage containing what looked like a ball of golden-brown fur, and a lively little beast who was pulling it about. Of course the ball was a sleepy little fellow who wanted to be let alone, and his cage-mate was trying to wake him up.

For a while the rolled-up creature endured the annoyance of his fellow, but on a harder push than usual, he slowly uncoiled a little, lifted his head, and looked up at me as if asking protection from all this pulling and hauling. Now I am susceptible to the pleading look in any dumb face, and that one was so innocent and mild, and the large eyes so intelligent, that my heart was won on the instant.

"What is that little brown beast?" I asked the man in attendance.

I was told that it was a night monkey, that a sailor had brought it from Africa as a pet, and they had bought it from him.

A night monkey! I had no desire for a monkey, full of pranks and mischief, in my houseful of birds, still less for one who would carry on his performances at night.

I turned away, but, giving one glance back, I was lost. The little fellow had come to the front of the cage, pulled himself up straight, and was looking at me in an earnest way that I could not resist. Without pausing to consider the difficulties to be overcome, I bought him at once, leaving him to be sent home the next day, and then I went home myself and worked out the problem of how to keep a night monkey in a parlor.

First, of course, I must have a cage, and this is what I planned, and had made. A tight box two feet square, of half-inch boards, with the whole front open. Over this open side a door of coarse-meshed wire gauze slid up and down. The bottom of the box was furnished with a zinc tray, with edges an inch high, on the top of which rested a slide of the same coarse wire gauze, and in the upper back corner was nailed a round wooden spicebox. I describe it thus carefully, to show my readers how easily a little beast may be accommodated in a parlor, and with how little care kept clean and sweet.

The wire floor, of course, let everything fall through into the tray under it, and thus the little fellow's fur was beautifully clean. To put the whole thing in order for the day was the work of five minutes. The zinc tray — on the bottom of which was always a sheet of newspaper — was drawn out, the newspaper carpet with its con-tents dumped bodily into the ash barrel, the tray held a moment under the hot-water faucet in the laundry, and thoroughly scalded. It was then dried, a fresh sheet of paper laid in it, and returned to the cage. All this in the morning, while the resident of the cage was rolled up in his blankets fast asleep, and thus it was left fresh and nice for the day.

He was a cold little beastie, and I feared at

first that we should never make him comfortable, although he was clad in a coat of thick wool, which stood out like the wool of a sheep, and would seem to be very warm. His cage, too, stood close to the register, and was covered all day by a thick double gray blanket. Yet he would not rouse himself at all, unless the thermometer stood at 78°, and to be lively he needed it at 80°. This was somewhat smothering to the family, but they heroically endured it for the pleasure the little African gave them.

All the long hours of daylight he passed simply as a ball of fur, deaf to all coaxing, oblivious alike of friend and foe; but during the night he was wide awake, and as full of life as any monkey.

Not being able to see in the dark easily, limits our acquaintances in the animal world, and among others, with all my efforts, I never knew my little pet as I wished, for light, even the dimmest, was a damper upon his freedom. I could listen to him, to be sure, and I did, through as many nights as I cared to give to it. What I heard was curious and suggestive, and I could fancy all sorts of performances, — turning of somersaults, dancing of jigs, queer pushing, shuffling, rustling, and gnawing, with straining of the joints of the cage, rattling of dishes, and now and then a fall to the floor, enough to break his bones.

Evidently he was my gentle pet no longer, but a wild beast trying to escape. Yet, even then, when his pranks were wildest, if I lifted the blanket and spoke to him, he quickly thrust out a cold hand to be warmed, and gently rubbed a soft nose against my hands, though two minutes after I left, the strange sounds were resumed.

The morning showed signs of his deeds : paper that had covered the floor torn to bits ; sawdust (which at first I kept on the bottom) scattered far and wide out on the carpet ; his much prized nest box gnawed, pulled from its fastening if possible, and upset on the floor ; water cup bottom up, and the cage flooded ; heavy woollen blanket that covered the door torn to ribbons, or made into " drawn work," more intricate than any designs in the pattern-book. These were the results that proclaimed his night's amusements. Woe to the household, I thought, if he succeeded in opening his door.

II

THE KINKAJOU AT HOME.

ON one occasion we had a guest, a lady who was afraid of the queer little fellow. During the night she was frightened by noises she heard in the parlor, and she declared that she heard a strange shuffling on the stairs, and a sniffing at her door.

I laughed at her, but when I entered the parlor I laughed no more. The room looked as if a cyclone had struck it. Vases were tipped over on a shelf; various articles of bric-à-brac were upset, a framed photograph thrown down, and even a framed engraving, quite heavy for so small a mischief maker, was lying on the floor, while books, work basket, and all small objects were scattered from one end of the room to the other.

Worse still, the author of all the confusion was not to be found. We searched the house from attic to cellar, in every spot he could hide; under the beds, behind the bureaus, and among the dresses in the closets. Fearing he had gone out at an open window, we even examined the roof, and the outside windowsills — no monkey to be found.

Grieving, both to lose him, and in dread of the fate he might meet in the streets of the city, I began to put the room in order, restore the pictures, which were not injured in any way, to their places, and pick up the scattered contents of my work basket. As I went to replace a volume in a set of low bookshelves, I caught sight of a bit of fur. I pulled out half a dozen books, and there, rolled into a snug ball, was the naughty rogue, fast asleep.

What did I do with him ? Why, I took hold of him, and he turned his sleepy eyes upon me with a look so innocent and winning that I put him back in his box, careful not to disturb his morning nap — and forgave him on the spot.

We never should have made the acquaintance of the odd little creature at all, if there had not been several hours between sundown and bedtime in which to study his curious ways. From the moment he aroused himself in the evening he was most interesting.

Soon after the gas was lighted and the family had become quiet, for he hated confusion or noise, his house was opened, by throwing the blanket portière over on to the top of the cage, and sliding up the wire door.

Before long the fur ball in the small round

box in the upper back corner began to uncoil,
two tiny hands appeared on the edge, followed
by a quaint little gray face, with a look so un-
canny that one could not wonder at the super-
stitions of the natives of his country about him.
First he looked over to make sure of his mistress, who always fed him. Then he leaned far
out of his box, taking hold of the water-cup
across the cage, and drawing his lithe body out
in a long, long stretch, bending his back downward like a bow turned the wrong way, opening
his mouth very wide, and thrusting out his curious tongue, which was very thin and reached
nearly three inches beyond his lips.

Then he drew back to his box, and proceeded
to get wide awake by stretching each limb sepa-
rately, and spreading the fingers wide apart.
Next came his toilet, for he was a well-mannered
little fellow, and never thought of coming to
breakfast till he was in perfect order.

His way of dressing was amusing. Over each
long limb he passed his claws, thoroughly combing the hair the wrong way, so that it must
perforce stand up; then lifting himself to an
upright position, resting on feet and tail, he
dressed the fur on his broad stomach, using both
hands in rapid alternation on the same spot, and
moving them so quickly and in so business-like
a manner that it was very funny to see. His

back and head were reached by one foot, or hand, in doing which he turned and twisted his arms and legs over his body, till it seemed as if he would dislocate the joints. His face he washed as a cat does hers, and he also washed other parts of his golden-brown fur, while covered up in his blanket, later in the evening; but the combing was the regular business, performed before he was ready for society.

This done he was ready for his supper — or should it be called breakfast, since he had eaten nothing later than the night before? A banana was peeled, a thin slice cut off, and offered to him on the point of a silver knife. He sniffed at it gently, above, below, on every side, and if exactly to his critical taste, he gravely opened his mouth and received it, every movement being with the utmost deliberation and dignity.

To eat it, he bit a piece off with the side teeth, threw back his head, and crushed it between the tongue and the roof of the mouth, which was crossed with bony-looking ridges. When he came to me he ate apples, but the first time he saw a banana he fairly snatched it with both hands, so that I could not get it away to peel for him. He tore the skin, and devoured it so greedily that he was furnished with bananas from that time.

Generally he ate sitting up like a kangaroo,

but when the piece was large, he sometimes lay
down on his back or side, and brought both
hands and feet into use for help. Occasionally,
if convenient, he sat up against a book, or stick
of wood, leaning on one elbow with a most sentimental air.

His position in sitting down was very curious.
So flexible was his body that he could sit down
at any point of his spine. He often bent at
about the middle of the back, while he slowly
dispatched his food; head and shoulders standing straight up without support, and the rest of
the body lying flat, with the two legs spread far
apart to keep the balance. Not unfrequently he
leaned over the edge of the box, back down,
eating, with his head hanging wrong side up,
in which position any other animal would break
his back.

Slice after slice of banana disappeared till
almost the whole of one was consumed, when
he coolly turned his back upon the tempter,
and curled down, apparently for a nap. But
this was merely a hint for people to withdraw,
resume their ordinary occupations, of book, or
work, or play, and leave him in freedom, which
they accordingly did.

MANNERS OF THE KINKAJOU.

THE coast being clear, as he ascertained by cautiously peeping out, the kinkajou, with great deliberation, prepared to come out for his evening promenade. First he reached over to the water-cup and refreshed himself with a drink, lapping it like a dog; then he quietly came to the floor of the cage with all fours, holding tightly to his nest by the long tail. Should any one move toward him then, he would scramble back into the nest, and curl down into the smallest possible space. But no one did ; and cautiously he moved about the cage, sniffing, or smelling, so vigorously that he might be heard across the room, and at last with perfect ease, although without haste, let himself down to the floor (about two feet), and started around the edge of the room.

At every chair he rose to an erect position, smelled at the cover, walking around it, and often taking two or three steps without holding on, showing that he had no difficulty in walking on two feet. Occasionally he pulled himself up

on to a chair, but he preferred the sofa. This
had a high back, which he quickly mounted,
running along the thin edge of carved wood, and
standing up on the highest point, to smell at a
picture frame on the wall.

Sometimes he curled down on the sofa for a
nap, but usually he proceeded with his tour of
the room, climbing the tall easel to the top, and
there standing up to reach still higher; sliding
down again by twining his tail around, and
clasping with his four little hands the back
support; inspecting the bell-pull, and trying to
understand the mystery of the speaking tube.

The kinkajou's tail was an interesting member, plainly for use more than ornament. As
he walked along the floor it dragged over everything with a sort of clinging feeling, and if
it touched anything, like the leg of a chair, it
curled around it. It was a great help in standing up, and in steadying his body when climbing. It was partly if not fully prehensile.

The little creature was very deliberate in his
usual movements, hobbling around the room like
a small bear, his long hind legs and turned-in
toes giving him a peculiarly awkward gait;
climbing tables and chairs, and coming down
head first in a cautious manner. If startled, he
galloped clumsily back to his corner, scrambled
into the cage, pulled himself up to his nest,

THE KINKAJOU

curled down out of sight, and stayed there till all was quiet again.

His round spice-box nest, eight inches in diameter, was his delight — by day to sleep in, and by night to tear to pieces. Now spice boxes are not very costly, but they come in sets, and with each one of the proper size came several smaller ones ; so, after overstocking my kitchen pantry and filling all my empty shelves, I put an end to the fun by getting a grocer's measure of the right size. This, being very thick, of hard wood and iron bound, was too much for his teeth, and when fastened by screws to a pair of iron brackets, defied all his attempts to destroy it. The blankets to sleep on and to keep him warm were lashed to the box ; else they would not be in place five-minutes.

Fond as the kinkajou was of his nest, when the door was open he discovered a place he liked even better. This was the top of his cage, four feet from the floor, where during the evening lay a thick double gray blanket, into the folds of which he delighted to creep, and peep out at us, when the room was cooler than he liked. To reach this snug retreat, he climbed an arm-chair which stood beside it, pulling himself first up to the seat, then to the arm, and then the back. When the room was of a temperature to please him, and consequently intolerable to us, he liked to lie outside the blanket in the oddest attitudes; sometimes flat on his back, with legs stretched to their utmost, sometimes on his stomach, with head hanging over the edge, in a way to break his neck, one would think. Head down was always a favorite attitude with him, and in the beautiful ball he made of himself it was not only turned down, but completely covered in the most smothering way.

The positions into which the kinkajou put his incredibly lithe body were marvelous; it often looked as though he had not a bone under his skin. He could bend his back in a perfect bow either way, turn and twist arms and legs into any impossible position, flatten himself to creep under a low bookcase, or narrow himself to pass between two books on a shelf. Any place where he could hold on was perfectly satisfactory. He sat on the sharp edge of a spice-box with all four feet (or hands) side by side, and so comfortably, that if he wished to eat he removed one hand for the purpose, and balanced himself easily on three, while he disposed of his lunch.

On one occasion, passing from a small table to the top of a cold stove a foot away, he had put one hand and one foot on the stove, but before releasing his hold of the table, decided to eat the slice of banana he held in the other hand ; so, all attitudes being equally agreeable, he simply rested there, one foot on the table and the tail laid across it, holding on to the further edge, and one foot and one hand on the stove. In this strange, unnatural position he remained, eating with the utmost deliberation, and washing his hands before he passed on. The stride of his hind limbs was remarkable. Climbing from the top of a chair to the mantel, ten or twelve inches away, and as much higher, he put up two hands and then one foot beside them before letting go of the chair. Then he did not jump, but pulled himself up.

His preparations for sleep were no less peculiar. He often curled his tail from the tip into a perfectly regular coil, which he used for a cushion, sitting upon it, and letting his pretty little finger-like toes hang over the edge ; but if he wished to sleep, he placed his face on this cushion, put his hands around and over, or tucked them in behind his head, and drew the long hind legs and feet up around the whole, making a complete ball. Sometimes when on the floor he curled the tail around outside. This was his favorite attitude for sleeping through the day.

IV.

THE KINKAJOU'S NAME AND HIS LOOKS.

To discover the name of my queer little pet, and his place in the books of Natural History, I found a hard task. Many volumes were studied, the search being based on the story I had been told, that he had come from Africa, and was called a night monkey.

In looks, habits, and manners he resembled the *Lemuridæ* or half-monkeys of that country. Books and traveled naturalists agreed that he must be a lemuroid, though no one could exactly place him. But one day, in looking for something else, I stumbled upon a description that suited him better than any other, and thus found that he was a kinkajou of Central and South America. It was plain, therefore, that somebody through whose hands he had passed had not the love of truth in his heart.

I was glad to find that I was not the first who had been puzzled by his resemblance to the lemurs. Naturalists have been uncertain where to place him, but at last have decided that he belongs to the bears, and his proper name is *Cercoleptes caudivolvulus*, though the South

Americans call him kinkajou, and the natives of Central America, conyeuse.

My little South American was one of the most nervous and observing creatures I ever saw; not a movement or a sound escaped his notice when awake. He would lie on my shoulder or the back of a chair by the hour, and watch the shadows — especially his own — as they fell on the carpet; he listened to the noises outside, cats, dogs, the elevated railroad, the latter with manifest disapproval.

He never liked to have any one come up behind him. A sudden noise startled him greatly, and his tiny hand had always a nervous jerk when I held it in mine. He had a most sensitive organization. At a distance, he liked to sit up and look at us, but if we moved to approach him, he turned his back, cuddled into a corner or buried his head under a blanket. It was not fear, for he readily came up on us, and, in fact, became troublesomely familiar at last.

He was playful in a quiet way. He amused himself with a string, as a kitten does, lying on his back and using all fours to toss it up and pull it around. In the same way he played with a long gold chain, biting and tossing it around, and he was extremely ticklish. His principal plaything was his own tail, which had a curious appearance of independent motion. It curled around his neck, laid itself over his eyes, or moved back and forth before his face, while he, lying on his back, seized it, pretended to bite and worry it. The card-table was wonderfully fascinating to him ; the cards he liked to put his sharp teeth into, and the cribbage pegs were simply irresistible.

The little animal was pretty as well as interesting ; about the size of a small cat, being fifteen inches from tip of nose to root of tail, with a furry, prehensile tail, sixteen inches long, which was always curled over at the tip. He had kinky wool, of a beautiful golden-brown color, darker on the back, with shining golden tips in the daylight ; this stood straight out all over his body excepting on the back of his hands, where it was silky and lay flat.

His hands, though without opposable thumbs, were beautifully shaped, with long, delicate fingers, webbed to the knuckles, with double joints, enabling him to bend them either way, and soft thick cushions or pads inside, so that he was shod with silence. His feet were exactly like his hands, excepting a heel-bone. Both hands and feet had long claws instead of nails, and were flesh-colored inside. His head was really beautiful, — shaped somewhat like a cat's, with a face of a grayish color ; he had delicate, sensitive ears, not large, but very wide open and movable with every emotion; his eyes were enormously large for his size, very full and prominent, black and gentle in expression, and over the inner corner of each was a little tuft of hair like a cat's whiskers, about an inch and a half long.

He had also whiskers on the sides of his nose like a cat's and another tuft of similar length under the chin. His nose was bare, and the nostrils were the peculiar shape of the lemur's. His tongue was of great length, and very thin, for what purpose I could not discover. Some writers say that it is to collect insects from crevices in bark, while others affirm that it is to gather honey stored away by bees. I could not induce my pet to touch any insect I could find, and he did not show fondness for sweets.

Stealthy movement and almost entire silence were characteristic of the kinkajou. In all the time he lived with us, we seldom heard a sound from him. Once, when accidentally hurt, he uttered a chattering sound like nothing so much as that made by a stick drawn across a picket fence, at the same time showing his teeth like a snarling dog; also, he repelled strangers with a rough breathing, a sort of " huff." When asleep, we sometimes heard from under the blanket where he lay, a low "yap" like a dreaming puppy's, or a whine like a dog's. Save these few times, he never uttered a sound.

V.

THE LAST OF THE KINKAJOU.

As time passed, and he became better acquainted and lost all fear, the little kinkajou became more affectionate and sociable. Especially so with his particular friend and mistress, to whom he had always shown partiality. In his wildest days, he would always put one soft hand, sometimes two of them, through the wires to be held, or to seize a finger to lick. He liked to have me hold my face near the wires, and let him put his hands on it. Almost every moment that he was out he insisted on being upon me, — my lap, my arm, or, best of all, my shoulder, where he would lie at full length, head outwards, to watch the room, with his tail around my neck as an anchor. Nor did he lie quiet even there. One moment he would suddenly turn and lick my cheek; then, as unexpectedly, would he take a gentle nip at my ear; and first and last and always jerk at my hair, which he seemed to regard as made for him to pull down, tangle, and play with.

Of this he made a business, standing on my shoulder, putting both hands on my head, and settling himself for a good frolic. What he wished to accomplish I never found out, for no one could long endure the rough treatment. If I succeeded in keeping him off my shoulder, he would establish himself on my arm, which he clasped with all four limbs, and held on for dear life, while he licked or playfully bit my hand or wrist. To shake him off was utterly impossible; he had a wonderful grip, and the more one shook, the closer he held.

As the weather grew warm, this little fur boa was not so comfortable around the neck; neither did I enjoy the warm little body glued to my arm; but it was impossible to get relief. If I put him down, or upon some one else for a rest, he would climb about and amuse himself till I made some movement or spoke, when instantly his quaint little face turned, he abandoned all else and ran for me. When I made violent effort to drive him away, pushing or in any way exciting him, he never was scared away; the more he was alarmed, the more frantically he would run for me, clamber up my chair, and mount to my shoulder as though that were his haven of refuge. The more I disturbed and pushed and tried to shake him off, the tighter he clung, and the more persistently he returned. Sometimes, when particularly affectionate, he threw all four arms (or legs) around my head so as completely to embrace it, and buried his teeth in my hair.

Trying to retain him on my lap by keeping the room still and never relaxing vigilance for a moment, if any sudden noise, a laugh, a door opened, or anything startled him, he would slip through my hands in spite of my efforts to hold him, scramble to my shoulder, throw his tail and perhaps an arm around my neck, and hold closely enough nearly to choke me.

This soon became intolerable. I could neither read nor do anything, except devote myself entirely to the kinkajou. I went away from home for a month — this was June — and during that time he never cared to come out of the cage. When the door was opened for evening, he would glance gravely out, sniff loudly, and look slowly around the room, then, in a few moments, curl down again to sleep. I hoped he was cured of his troublesome fondness, but on my return he came out at once, and proceeded to amuse himself and torment me in the same old way.

The weather was now very warm, and I could not endure his embarrassing attentions. I would not keep him confined to his cage, so I presented him to the National Museum at Washington, where he was not so gentle and amiable as he had been with us, but bit and scratched, and, in fact, went quite back to savagery.

VI.

A KINKAJOU IN A BOARDING SCHOOL.

A KINKAJOU whose story was told to me by his mistress was for four days a pet in a girls school in Central America. Although a native of that country, he is rarely seen, because of his habit of making the night his playtime, and the people are rather in awe of him.

This one used to sleep all day, rolled into a ball in some corner, sometimes even on the window-sill in the schoolroom. When in that position, he might be tumbled all about the floor without waking, or at least without uncoiling.

For his breakfast, he sat up in a child's little chair and, holding a banana in each hand, took a bite from each in turn till he had enough. Then he simply opened his fingers, and let the fruit drop, and fell to washing his hands with great care. Unlike my pet, he breakfasted before he dressed his fur, but he combed and brushed himself up very nicely afterward.

The greatest part of his enjoyment consisted in examining the strange things he found about him, and pulling them to pieces to see how they were made. Nothing escaped his busy fingers, and scarcely anything could resist his sharp nails.

He was a social and warmth-loving creature, and desired above all things to be in somebody's lap. And he was so droll in his way of getting about, and so deliberate in his movements, that his mistress never tired of watching him.

But when the family went to bed at ten o'clock, his day, of course, was just beginning, and as he was not caged, he found the field open for him to indulge his taste for investigation.

His first prank was to tear to pieces a whole banana plant. The severest cyclone that ever passed over a prairie in the West could not more completely demolish a tender plant than his four little hands did.

Great was the outcry when the family came out in the morning, and saw how he had amused himself during his first night in the house.

But when they looked for the culprit, and found the little bundle of fur on the corner of a window-sill, and roughly shook him out, prepared to punish him severely, the calm, innocent look in the sleepy eyes he turned upon them disarmed them instantly, as the same look in my own pet always did me. The fiercest wrath vanished. " Poor little beastie ! " they said, " how did he know it was mischief ? " and he was forgiven and laid gently down again to sleep.

The second night — grown wiser, as they thought, and resolved that no more plants should suffer — they shut him up in a school-room. With nothing but desks and benches, he could surely do no harm.

Could he not? They thought differently the next morning, when they went in and found the costly " solar system," without which no child could be expected to understand how the earth and the moon and the various planets perform their several waltzes around the sun, a total ruin, as hopelessly destroyed as the banana plant had been, and the little beast again coiled up, sleeping the sleep of innocence.

His owner grew sober; if this was his way of passing the night, it would soon empty her purse to pay for his fun. But he was so droll, she could not bring herself to give him up. She would try him again. The next night, accordingly, he was carefully shut out of the school-room, lest he try his hand on the benches themselves, for by that time they began to think he could do anything he chose.

With no fun on hand he became lonely, and started on a search after society, which he always liked, but seldom enjoyed, since everybody was in bed through most of his waking hours.

On this unlucky occasion the principal of the school, who was so nervous as to faint at a spider, and who of course "hated pets," happened to be engaged in some writing, which kept her up after the rest of the household had retired. In that warm climate, the bedrooms all open upon the corridor, and have, for hot nights, slat doors, high enough to keep people out, but not reaching the top of the door frame.

The kinkajou saw a chance of company; so, calmly and silently, in the stealthy way of his race, he climbed over the slats and surprised the late worker by a leap on to her lap. He was greeted with a wild shriek, which awoke everybody in that part of the house. Then, while his mistress lay waiting in terror for what should happen next, she heard muffled steps without, a sudden movement, and a heavy fall on her floor. She sprang up, got a light, and found her naughty pet, much surprised but not hurt, thanks to the soft cushions of his feet and his cat-like way of falling upon them. His greatly offended enemy had throw him over the slat door!

The next day the principal looked rather sober, though she said nothing, and his mistress began to consider what she could do with him to prevent further trouble. But that night, the fourth of his residence with her, he took his fate

into his own hands, and settled his sentence of
banishment.

He wandered into the dormitory where twenty
boarders in as many beds were sleeping the
sound sleep of schoolgirls. What the poor little
fellow did could never be found out, probably
no one knew exactly; but he made his presence
obvious in some way, and startled one girl out
of sleep. Her shrieks threw nineteen more into
a panic of terror, that ended — when the family
had rushed in half dressed, and the cause of the
uproar was discovered — in a fit of hysterics all
around.

Solemnly and grimly the principal sent for
a bottle of bromide, and sternly she forced every
girl to take a dose, while the kinkajou's mistress
gathered the naughty little beast into her arms
and meekly retired to her own room.

That night she sat up and entertained the
troublesome pet, and the next day he was
returned to the hand that gave him, with the
verdict that he was exceedingly interesting, but
his manners needed cultivation to fit him for
general society.

II.

LIVING BALLS.

MANY animals have the power of rolling themselves into a ball, not only to sleep, but for
protection from enemies stronger than themselves, with whom they could not fight. Perhaps
the most interesting of these is a little-known
animal of South America, the ball armadillo, or
— in the books — the *Dasypus apar*.

This creature, scarcely more than a foot long,
is nearly covered by a horny case, curiously
divided into six-sided plates, with three bands
around his body. He looks funny enough when
walking about, exactly as if he had a decorated
blanket over him held in place by three girdles.
Over his wide face, almost hiding his eyes, is a
pointed shield of the same horny substance, and
another protects the top of his short tail.

This queer fellow delights in turning himself
into a ball. If he is in the least afraid of
anything, or if a friend is too rough, he rolls up
with a snap, like a spring, and sometimes the
rough-handed friend gets his fingers nipped between the sharp edges of his case.

Nothing is so droll as two of these odd little creatures pretending to fight. The thing each one tries to do is to bite the ears of his opponent, or with his claws to tear the tough skin between the three bands. They scuffle without much ferocity till one gets a slight advantage, when, presto! snap! his enemy has become a ball, and a ball he patiently remains, in spite of the efforts of beast or man, till he has tired out his assailant, or considers it proper to unbend.

In this shape the armadillo is safe from the attacks of larger animals, with which he could not for an instant cope. The jaguar prowling through the woods in search of food may roll him about, but can neither crush him between his teeth nor force him open with his paw. Monkeys, which, true to their love of fun, delight in teasing small and harmless animals by pulling them around by the tail, look in vain for a tail to take hold of. It is not unlikely that he enjoys some lively rolling about at the hands of these frolicsome quadrumana, although no such performance has been reported. Only from man, who can take him up and carry him home to unroll at his leisure, is this no protection.

The apar is an interesting little beast apart from his habit of retiring within his shell. He is lively and playful, and therefore much liked as a pet. His walk is very odd. He has on the

fore feet three long claws, on the tips of which
he totters about, and on the hind feet five claws,
which he plants flatly on the ground.

It is curious that although many animals assume as nearly as possible a spherical shape in
sleeping, this little fellow, to whom that shape
is so familiar and easy, sleeps, on the contrary,
stretched out his full length, resting on the stomach, with fore paws laid together straight before
him, head flat between the two, and shield arched
up over him like a roof.

Bolita (little ball), as he is called by the natives, is said by some travelers to be as expert
at tunneling as at ball-making. His enormous
claws being admirable digging tools, he is able
to burrow in soft earth so rapidly that a man
can scarcely seize him before he is out of sight.
Underground, if still pursued, he continues his
tunnel, and to dig him out, even with all the
wit of man in saving labor, is the work of hours.

The ball armadillo is much sought for by the
natives to eat, though, when caught, his innocent,
attractive ways often change his destiny from
roasting in his own shell to being the cherished
household pet and playmate for the children,
whose romps and games with the pretty living
ball are various and charming to see.

The baby bolita is one of the drollest of infants, dressed from the first in armor complete

as that of his elders, but light in color, and soft
like parchment.

The Old World furnishes another living ball
in the manis, or scaly ant-eater. This strange
animal is about eighteen inches in length, with
a tail as long as the body, and a protecting
armor different from, but quite as effectual, as
that of the armadillo. From nose to tip of tail
the manis is clothed in gray horny scales, shield-
shape and convex, so that they lie closely, lapping over each other. The tail is very broad,
and possesses great muscles of such power that
several men together fail to move it from its
chosen position, wrapped around the ball he
makes of himself. In this position he is quite
different from the armadillo. Instead of offer-
ing a smooth, hard surface to the enemy, each
plate stands up from the rest, all presenting an
array of sharp, horny points extremely unpleasant to the touch of man or beast. To assume
the ball shape he places his head between the
fore legs, wraps the tail over legs and head,
bringing it up on to the neck, and there he holds
it, while leopards and jackals, as well as men,
try their strength on him in vain.

The manis is quite as odd when walking about
as the armadillo, though not in the same way.
The claws of his fore feet being long and curved,
he turns them under or back, and walks on the

outside of them, holding his back highly arched as he goes. He has also a curious manner of standing erect on his hind legs for a better view of things, using his broad tail to balance himself.

A better known animal of ball-making habits is the common hedgehog, of whose spine-covered, impervious ball we have all read from childhood, if we have not seen. He also, like the armadillo, resorts to the spherical form in time of war. When " having it out " with a venomous snake, for instance, he will give a savage bite on the back, and instantly retire behind or within his sharp spines, which, projecting on all sides, effectually keep the reptile at a safe distance. After a time he will cautiously unroll and take an observation, and, if the snake is off its guard, give another sudden bite, and so on till he breaks the back. In the same way he protects himself from dogs, which are loath to attack the spiny ball.

Not only as a safeguard from enemies is this accomplishment useful to the hedgehog, but as a protection from other perils. Should he lose his hold and fall from a height, even of twenty feet, he instantly pulls himself together into a ball, and reaches the ground unhurt. It is even said that he often chooses that easy way, and deliberately throws himself to the ground, rather than take the trouble to climb.

The largest animal known to assume the ball shape for safety is the black bear of the Himalayas, called also the Tibetan sun-bear, and about the size and color of our American black bear. When pursued by hunters in his mountain home, he will draw himself up into a large ball of fur, and deliberately roll down the steep hillsides, bounding off the rocks, and of course reaching the valley much more quickly than any hunter who cannot follow his short cut. At the bottom he simply unrolls, shakes himself, and walks off at his leisure.

The strangest animal in the world, perhaps, is the duck-bill platypus of Australia, and rolling himself into a ball is one of his dearest delights. An English naturalist who kept a pair of these curious fellows alive, to study their ways, made drawings of the different shapes they put themselves into, and their common sleeping position he found to be that of a ball. To get himself into this form, the animal placed the fore paws under the beak, bending its head downward ; it then laid the hind paws over the mandibles and lastly turned the tail up over all, to make the whole complete, when it looked like a well-made fur ball. The naturalist was able to draw down the tail, and thus disclose the method of packing ; but unless the creature was sound asleep it would growl like a savage puppy.

His account of the manners of his strange
pets is very readable. Like other young animals, they were extremely playful, and their
antics, being like those of puppies, were most
ludicrous in creatures so oddly shaped as the
Ornithorhynchus. The toilet after bathing was
of great interest. In this operation they used
the claws of the hind feet alone, twisting the
body easily in several directions, changing feet
when tired, and picking the fur as a bird dresses
its feathers. Even the head was combed by the
claws of the hind feet, and after an hour of this
work, the little creatures were beautifully sleek
and glossy.

Another ball-maker is the koala or Australian
native bear. He is a most attractive little beast,
not much bigger than a cat, clothed in long ashy
gray fur. His short face, with its large black
eyes and nose and the long hairy decorations of
his ears, gives him a quaint expression. He rolls
himself up to sleep, and when awake the droll
black-haired baby travels about perched on the
shoulders of his mamma, and makes a charming
picture to look at.

Nearly every part of the world furnishes a
ball - maker. In Africa is found one of the
strangest of beasts, the galago, belonging to the
Lemur family. There are several species, some
the size of a rat, and others as large as a cat,

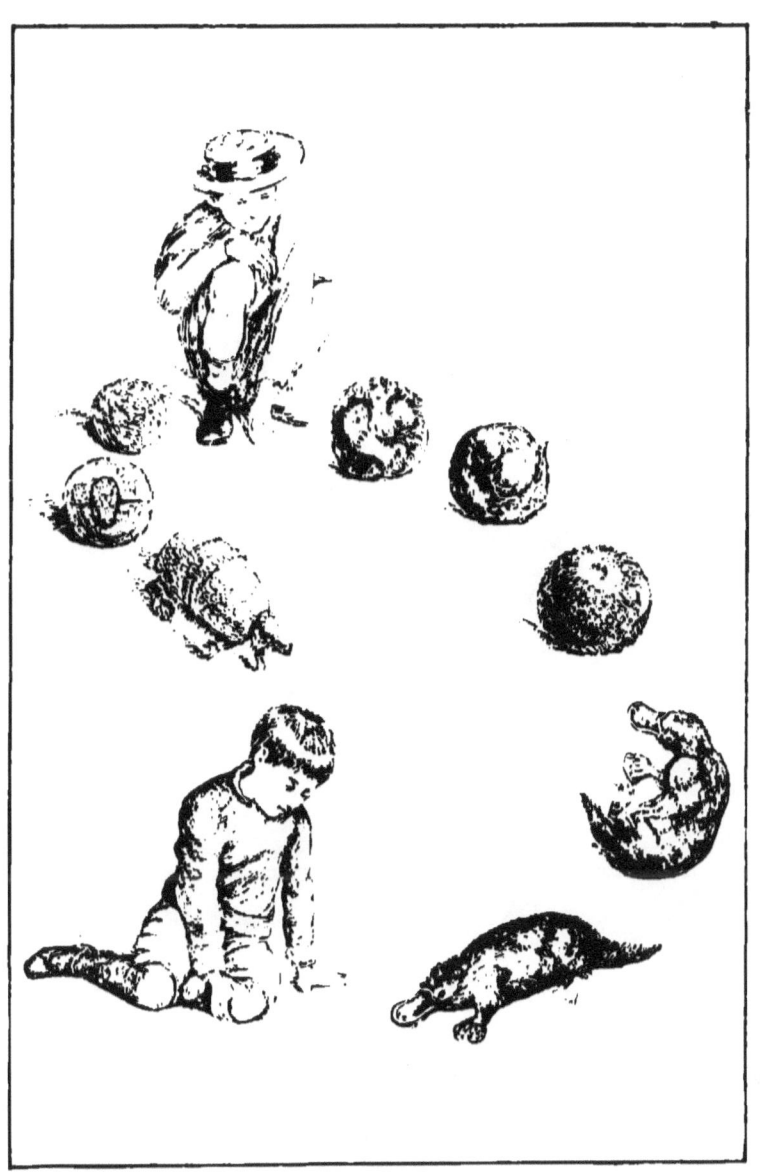

THE ARMADILLO AND DUCK-BILL

but their manners and habits are about the same.

They are, like the kinkajou, night - lovers. During the day they prefer to sleep, rolled up into a ball, but at night they are as full of pranks as a monkey. They will jump about, holding themselves upright like a kangaroo, from the floor to a table, or to a person's shoulder, sometimes uttering a loud cry, or a lively chattering, and again going about in perfect silence.

The galagos are pretty little creatures with woolly fur and very long bushy tails, and they are four-handed. They have great staring eyes, as night-loving creatures are apt to have, and their ears are curious, very large, and capable of being folded or drawn down so as to be almost closed, — a convenient arrangement for fellows who want to sleep all day. Some of them have been kept as pets, and others in museums, and they are very entertaining.

The island of Madagascar contributes to the ball-making beasts one of the strangest animals in the world, the aye-aye. He is also of the Lemur family, and so shy and solitary in his habits that even the natives of the country are not familiar with him.

All day long, when other animals and men are wide awake, he sleeps rolled into a ball

among the thickest bunches of leaves, on the
bamboos, in the deepest woods. But when the
day-lovers have gone to bed, the queer little
beast comes out to frolic and to eat. He eats
the pith of bamboos and sugar-canes, and is fond
of beetles and grubs as well, and he makes more
noise than the galago, uttering a sort of plain-
tive cry as he jumps from branch to branch.

He is a singular-looking animal, with large
eyes and ears, and a tail longer than his body.
His fur is bushy and long, and very dark in
color. But the most remarkable things about
him are his hands. The hinder pair are like
other lemurs, but the front ones have the strangest bony fingers of different lengths, the second
one so long and thin that it looks like a bent
wire.

For a long time no one knew the use of this
remarkable finger, but at last a naturalist kept
one alive and watched him. In his cage was
put at one time a worm-eaten branch, and when
the captive came out at dusk he at once began
to examine it. With his wire-like finger he
gently tapped the bark, at the same time holding his large ears close to it, listening.

Finally he seemed to hear something that
pleased him, for at once he began to tear off the
bark with his strong teeth, and to cut into the
wood, till he reached the entrance to a nest

where a grub was snugly lying. Then he thrust in his slender finger and brought out the choice morsel, which he ate with great relish.

When the aye-aye drinks he uses the strange finger in another way; holding his open mouth conveniently near, he scoops or throws the water into it, so rapidly that it seems to rush in in a stream.

It is said that this queer little fellow lives in a nest which he makes of the long leaves of the "traveler's tree," rolled up, and lined with dry leaves. It is ball-shaped, with an opening in one side, and is placed in a fork in a large tree.

III.

THE HALF-MONKEY.

I. KOKO.

Many a strange little beast from far-off quarters of the globe may be picked up in New York, in places where sailors are wont to dispose of their pets. In such a place I found and bought a rare and interesting animal, a black-headed lemur, or *Lemur brunneus*, native of Madagascar. He was a member of my household for nearly a year, and during that time the family circle was never dull. The whole of Barnum's menagerie next door could not have afforded more entertainment than did this one droll little fellow.

He was about the size of a small cat, or, to be exact, from the tip of his pointed nose to the root of the tail he measured sixteen inches; of that length, three inches were face and thirteen body and neck. His girth back of the fore legs was nine inches.

The manners of the little stranger were extremely odd. His home was the cage in the parlor already described, where he was generally alone all day, and spent the time, it is to be supposed, in sleeping, although I must admit I rarely found him so. At about four in the afternoon I went into the room and let him out. The moment I appeared he came to the front of the cage, pressed his weird little black face with its clear topaz eyes to the wires, and then began to call and "weave" impatiently. The latter was a singular movement. Planting his hind legs far apart, he held up, and outward, his short arms, and swayed his whole body from side to side, at each end of his swing bringing his hands down almost to the floor. This he did very rapidly, uttering every moment a short, quick sort of double grunt, with an occasional explosion or "snort," in the exact tone of a pig.

Of course I instantly opened his door, from that time till ten o'clock being his regular daily outing. Like a flash he bounced through it, jumped to the nearest chair, from that to the sofa, the table, somebody's lap or shoulder, the mantel, the top of his cage, or the piano, and so made the circuit of the two parlors, without touching the carpet.

After thus going the grand rounds, he generally jumped to the floor, and ran all about under the furniture. His sharp nose nearly touched the carpet, and his back (owing to the four inches difference in length between his fore

and hind limbs) sloped up at an angle of forty-
five degrees to the tail, which stood straight up
like a banner over his back, the tip sometimes
curling forward like a dog's, sometimes backward like a hook. During the whole performance he constantly uttered a contented single
grunt like "woof!"

If any movement in the room startled him, he
broke into a grotesque gallop, bringing his feet
up closely beside his hands at every leap. This
gallop, which was rapid and light, always ended
in a sudden spring to somebody's lap, or a
scramble to the top of a tall easel, where he
looked around to see what had frightened him.
But if not disturbed, when his tour of inspection
was over he usually went to the open fire, placed
himself sometimes on the toe of a lady's slipper
if it were conveniently near, sometimes on a little
three-by-five-inch cushion on the arm of an easy-
chair.

Here he sat up like a cat, with tail hanging
out before him, or fell eagerly to dressing his
peculiar woolly fur, which stood out all over his
body. He washed his face by licking the outside edge of his hand and rubbing it back and
forth over his face, and wiped his mouth on a
chair, as a bird wipes its bill, first one side and
then the other. Especially did he labor over his
eighteen-inch-long tail, scraping up the fur till

it stood straight out, and made that member look enormously large. The tool with which he accomplished so much was his curious row of lower front teeth, which ended in points almost as sharp as needles, and projected so much that they could not be used to bite, but made an effective scraper for the skin, or a comb for his own gray wool.

Warmed and dressed, the playful fellow began his evening's amusement. If the master's quiet game of cribbage was going on, he often began by springing without warning to the middle of the table, scattering cards like chaff, upsetting cribbage-board and sending the pegs flying, slapping cards out of the hands of the players and biting needle-like holes in them.

To make a great commotion of any sort was his delight. Sitting peacefully on my lap, or lying flat upon his stomach, every limb stretched out, apparently the most innocent and harmless of pets, he would often quietly rise to his feet, and, before I suspected him, snatch my book out of my hand or spring over it into my face. If I started at this rough salute, as I was tolerably sure to do, he was struck with panic, gave one mighty bound to the mantel, the bracket of a lamp, the edge of an open door, or the floor, where he stood a few seconds motionless as he alighted. A fright, indeed, always struck him with curious effect. Whether he was lying quietly on one's knee, standing, sitting, or in whatever position, on being alarmed by an attempt to capture him, or by an unexpected sound, he instantly disappeared, — sideways, backward, or forward, — without in any way making ready, or getting upon his legs. It was as if his body were a spring, or as if he were flung by some force outside of himself; he simply went. A curious fashion he had also of leaping against the bare side wall of the room, which he struck flatly with all fours, and then bounded off in another direction. I have seen the same thing done by a squirrel, and also — strange as it seems — by a bird.

MANNERS OF THE LEMUR.

THE extreme nervousness of the little lemur seemed to be caused by too much company. When alone with one person, especially if that one were my daughter or myself — his prime favorites — he was as quiet as the family cat. He sat or lay in the lap, and allowed himself to be brushed; indeed, he enjoyed brushing, and thrust out arms and legs to be operated upon. He sat up with his tail laid over his shoulders in a comical way; and, if he wanted to turn his head, he "ducked" it under the tail and brought it up the other side, rather than change its comfortable position. This member was really a great care to the little beast; he spent hours in dressing it, and by means of it he expressed all his emotions. When in quiet mood it hung straight down, as stiffly as if made of wood; if he were on mischief bent, it assumed a naughty-looking sidewise turn, though still hanging; during his pranks and in excitement it stood up like a flagstaff, safely out of harm's way; if his "angry passions rose," it was swished, after the manner of a cat; and when he jumped, it delivered a severe blow, like a smart rap with a stick.

Never was a living creature more alert than this small brute. So acute was his hearing that it was absolutely impossible to surprise him. No matter how quietly and apparently off his guard he sat on a chair, one could not jerk or tip that piece of furniture so quickly as to take him unawares; at the first sign of movement he appeared on the other side of the room, one could hardly tell how. I wanted much to see him when he did not see me, and to that end several times stole into the room from the front. The back of the cage was toward that side, and he could not possibly see me. I took off my shoes, and moved without the slightest sound over the carpet; but when I reached the point where I could see the open front of his cage, there he was, waiting, looking for me, his bright yellow eye pressed eagerly against the wires, in the corner nearest the side I came to. The instant he saw me he uttered a mocking grunt, which plainly said, "Thought you'd surprise me, eh?" and began a violent weaving and coaxing to get out.

Perhaps he was thus wide awake because he seemed really to fear being alone, and to dread the dark. The moment he was left in the room the spirit of mischief departed, and he retreated to the top of his cage, where he stayed till some one came in. The dusk, with its shadows, always alarmed him, and, when taken into a strange room, he cowered and clung to his friend as if frightened out of his wits. Fond as he was of society, he was exceedingly nervous about it. When he heard a person coming through the hall, he first ran to the end of a sofa nearest the door; as the steps approached, he grew more and more uneasy; and when the hand touched the door-knob, he yielded to wild panic, bounded to the other end of the sofa and over the back, where he held by one hand, while his body dangled behind.

His great sensitiveness showed also in another way; he never met a human eye with his own. He saw every expression of the face, but he always looked just beyond it. He violently objected to being stared at, turned his head away, and, if his head were held between two hands for the purpose of looking in his face, he got away, either by a sudden spring to the top of the head of his captor, or by wriggling himself out backward. His wool-covered body it was almost impossible to hold.

But although the little fellow would not look one squarely in the face, he saw everything that happened, and was as inquisitive as any monkey. He liked to sit before the window and look at passers-by, both beast and human; a cat he saluted by a short, sharp bark. A bugle that was brought out proved most interesting. He rose on his hind legs, which he did with perfect ease, and thrust his nose into the large end, evidently to find the sound. Once happening to get possession of it when its owner was absent, he made a thorough examination of it. He pulled it on to the floor, threw his body across it, embracing it with his legs to keep it in place, pushed his head almost out of sight into the big end, then took the small end in his mouth, as if to blow, and made minute and careful study of every part of it, until fully satisfied that whatever he sought was beyond his reach, when he threw it down and left it.

III

KOKO'S INTELLIGENCE.

THE intelligence of the lemur was notable. He knew his own blankets instantly, wherever he saw them, and was quite positive that no one had a right to touch them; he learned his name readily, always answered when spoken to, and came at a call like a dog, which animals of his sort rarely do. He also knew his own box, his chosen seats, his place before the fire, and insisted that they should not be used by others. In pictures he recognized a bird, tried to snatch it out of the paper, as he did also any figures that looked like insects. He disapproved of change, complained when I closed the shutters, and looked askance at me when I put on a different dress. He knew with perfect certainty who would let him out of the cage and who would not; one of the gentlemen of the house might sit in the parlor all day, and, except for keeping an eye on him, the little beast made no sign; but let either of his mistresses enter, and he was excited at once, weaving, grunting, and demanding that the door be opened. He understood at once, too, when forbidden to do anything.

On the occasion of the visit of a child, he was at first very jealous; did not like her to occupy a lap he had considered his own, and opposed with a squealing grunt her sitting on his special stool before the fire. But she was a gentle child, and a little later he became very fond of her, let her pat him, sit beside him on his seat, and at last insisted upon lying on some article of her dress, if any were in the room.

What the small African set his mind on, he always secured in the end, for his persistence was simply marvelous. He was as fond of apples as any schoolboy, and the head of the family liked to tantalize him by coming in with one hidden in his pocket. The sharp little nose sniffed it at once, and the eager little fellow sprang upon the apple-bearer, tried to dive into his pocket head first, then to dig into it from below, and, despairing of this, went to work to tear away the garments that covered it. No doubt he would have succeeded, but before he went so far the owner gave in, and handed the fruit to the impatient creature. He snatched it at once, and fairly "gobbled" it, biting off pieces with his back teeth, throwing his head up to chew them, and carefully separating and dropping the skin.

He never at any time made a full meal, as do many beasts. His desire seemed to be merely to stop the cravings of hunger; the moment this was done he opened his hand, and whatever food was in it dropped to the floor. He ate bread, sweet potato, and banana, and drank milk and water; but his delight was candy, and that he never dropped. If there was a bit in sight he was simply wild. When a piece was offered, he snatched it, chewed it down, and instantly begged for more. The favorite trick of a mischievous youth was to give him a licorice-drop, which became soft in the mouth, held his jaws together, and in every way was troublesome; but, in spite of his struggles with it, he was never discouraged, and always coaxed for another.

No beast that I ever saw was more fond of play than the little Malagasy, not even a lively kitten. From the moment his door was opened till he was shut in for the night, he generally gave his mind to a constant succession of pranks. He scraped the beads off our dress-trimmings with his comb-like teeth, and he slapped or pulled books or work out of our hands. He especially liked to frolic in one's lap, lying on his back, kicking with all fours, pretending to bite, and even turning somersets, or giving the most peculiar little leaps. To do this he flung out his arms, dropped his head on one side in a bewitching way, turned half around in the air, and came down in the spot he started from, the whole performance so sudden, and his face so grave all the time, it seemed as if a spring had gone off inside of him, with which his will had nothing to do.

A favorite plaything with the lemur was a window-shade. He began by jumping up to the fringe, seizing it and swinging back and forth. One day he learned by accident that he could " set it off," and then his extreme pleasure was to snatch at it with so much force as to start the spring, when he instantly let go and made one bound to the other side of the room, or to the mantel, where he sat, looking the picture of innocence, while the released shade sprang to the top and went over and over the rod. We could never prevent his carrying out this little programme, and we drew down one shade only to have him slyly set off another the next instant.

Next to the shade, his chosen playground was a small brass rod holding a bracket-lamp. It was not more than half an inch wide, and so sharp-edged that it seemed impossible that an animal of his size and weight could stay on it one minute, especially as it was not more than eight or ten inches long, and held a burning lamp at the end. The lamp was no objection to the always chilly little beast; he enjoyed the heat of it, and not only did he sit there with perfect ease, and dress his fur or eat his bread, but he played what seemed impossible pranks on it. He turned somersets over it; he hung by one hand and swung ; he jumped and seized it with hand or foot ; whisked over it, and came up the other side. He never made a slip nor touched the lamp, and his long, stiff tail served as a balancing pole.

IV

PRANKS OF A PET.

PERHAPS the greatest fun our little captive had was with a newspaper. The thing that first interested him was being told to let it alone when he longed to tear it up. This desire of his kept us always on the watch for our papers, till at last I resolved to give him his wish. I took an old paper, and put it on the floor for him.

First he came with a big leap into the middle of it, when the rustle instantly scared him off, in a second bound as tremendous as the first. He soon came back, however, and began again. He turned somersets on it, rolled over it, then took hold of one corner and rolled himself up in it. But all the time every fresh rustle of the paper put him in a panic, and he leaped spasmodically away. It was a wild frolic impossible to describe, with attitudes so comical, movements so unexpected, and terror and joy so closely united, that it was the funniest exhibition one can imagine.

The next evening I arranged a newspaper tentwise on the floor. The lemur looked at it sharply, examined the tempting passage-way

under it, then dashed frantically through, and
flew to the highest retreat in the room, as if he
had taken his life in his hands. He returned —
for it was impossible to keep away — and resumed his gambols, his hand-springs, his various
fantastic exercises; and between each two antics
flung himself about the room as if he had gone
mad, ending every romp by sitting a few seconds
motionless, with a grave and solemn air, as if it
were out of the question that he could be guilty
of anything frivolous.

Early in his residence with us, he made up his
mind that free use of the two mantels in the
rooms he had the run of was desirable. Those
shelves being already occupied, the family naturally opposed his wish. In vain. Every point
in his advance he won with a struggle; chairs
were removed to a distance and reproofs show-
ered upon him. All wasted effort. To frolic
upon those mantels was his aim, and he secured
it. We gave up at last, pushed the bric-a-brac
against the wall, and let him enjoy his victory,
but we might have spared ourselves the fight,
for he never did the slightest harm.

Most amusing were his acrobatic feats on a
set of clothes-bars, brought from the laundry for
his use. He accepted the enticing array of
small rods three quarters of an inch in diameter,
without a doubt that it was intended for him, as

in fact he did everything; that he could be un-
welcome anywhere never occurred to him. The
moment the bars were set up, he made one flying
leap across the room and landed upon them.
He ran all over those small sticks as if they
were a level floor, using his tail as a balancing
pole; he turned hand somersets (if I may call
them so) over them; hung from one or both
feet, head down and arms stretched out, and in
this attitude often washed his face. He flung
himself from one post to another, never missing
his hold, though the whole thing shook and
creaked with his violence. He went up the corner post hand over hand, using all fours, and
stood upright on the top, looking up for more
worlds to conquer. One moment he swung by
his hands, his long legs drawn up, and the next
he seized a bar with the right hand and foot, and
whirled over it, coming up in the same position,
a sort of side somerset. There was nothing
possible to a monkey that he did not do, and I
never saw a monkey half so lively. The little
fellow was so happy, and we so entertained, that
the clothes-bars became for a time a part of the
parlor furniture.

The bars, too, helped Koko to solve a problem that he had been revolving since he first
came to us. He longed to explore the top of a
tall old-fashioned bookcase, as we knew by his

eager looks and movement, threatening to jump
up from the back of a chair. In his antics one
day he sprang over to the upright window-casing, to examine an ornament of moss that hung
on the wall, and the ease with which he held
on to the moulding put another notion into his
head. He had found a ladder! — and he began
to climb.

This discovery removed the last obstacle between Koko and everything in the room. With
three long windows, a wide arch, and a door, all
surrounded by this highway of ladders, he could
reach almost anything on the walls hitherto
barred from him. The first thing, of course,
was to gratify his old longing to explore the
bookcase : he walked up the moulding till he was
level with the top, and then jumped over the
chasm. In about two minutes he satisfied himself that nothing was there but dust, and having
well covered his feet and hands with this, he
sprang back to the casing and ran down, leaving pretty little prints of his mischievous hands
all the way. After that exploit the casings were
his favorite playground and retreat.

V

MORE LEMUR WAYS.

A GREAT pleasure to Koko when there was no fire was to sit on the centre-table, close to a big Rochester-burner lamp, and luxuriate in its heat. The first time he tried this seat, he put one inquisitive finger on the shade, but instantly thrust it into his mouth with a glance at me. I laughed at him, and, feeling insulted, he ran out his tongue, and saluted me with a mocking " Ya ! ya ! ya ! " Often as he sat there afterward he never touched the lamp again.

When a fire was burning in the open stove, a foot-rest was placed before it for the use of the little beast, who spent many hours there. Sometimes he sat with his tail around his neck like a boa, but usually he was bolt upright with his feet stretched out toward the fire, while he dressed the hair of his tail, which was several inches longer than his body and an object of great care. His way of doing this was to haul it up before his face, and hold it with both hands, while he washed and combed it the wrong way ; that is, so that the hair stood up instead of lying down. His hair was woolly and not soft,

KOKO AT PLAY

and this treatment of course made it stand out all over, forming a very pretty coat, and a thick cushion around him. By this process his tail, after he was kept nicely, was made to look very large; as I said before, near the root it became fully three inches in diameter.

A seat Koko liked very much, was the top of a high rocking-chair, a bamboo rod an inch and a quarter in diameter. In spite of the most violent rocking, he had no trouble to keep his place, holding on with all four hands side by side, or by two hands on the post at one end. In this place he dressed his fur or washed his face, with perfect ease and calmness. In fact, so sure was his hold that to get him off a person was almost impossible; he could not be shaken from an arm, for instance; he clasped both arms and legs tightly around it, and no jar or pull would remove him.

We did learn a trick after a while that always sent him with a leap to the floor, where he stood and looked at his tormentor with a reproachful expression, sometimes ran his tongue out very rapidly several times, as children do to show contempt, and then went back, with a forgiving spirit that usually won him the place again. This potent spell was an imitation of his own "woof!" The instant it was uttered, he sprang off without rising to his feet, or turning his head to see where he should alight. The cushions under his fingers and toes, indeed, made it a matter of indifference where he did fall; he could not hurt himself.

Troublesome was the position of " best friend " to the little fellow, for whatever happened to him, if he got into mischief, if any one spoke reprovingly to him, if he was suddenly startled, he went on a mad gallop for his friend, sprang to her knee, to her shoulder, to the top of her head if she would allow it, and from that point turned upon his enemy, ready to defend himself.

He could be very savage, too; he had sharp teeth, and a ferocious way of resenting a direct insult. He flew at the enemy, screaming with rage, climbed up his clothes (it was always man or boy), and acted as if he would tear him to pieces. But the fury was short-lived ; in a few moments he grew calm, though I think he never lost suspicion of a person who had once ill-treated him.

One thing that Koko considered an unpardonable affront was an exclamation sometimes used to drive away strange cats, a sort of "quish!" spoken with emphasis. This always infuriated him. If reproved by any one excepting the two ladies of the household, in those highly offensive words " No ! no !" he was displeased also, turned suddenly, looked over at the speaker with a squeal which plainly expressed the opinion that it was not his business to interfere. When either of his special friends used the same words, he instantly turned to her, galloped across the room, and bounded on to her shoulder.

Koko was not dependent on outside objects for his amusement; he bubbled over with fun, and his whimsical little pranks can never be half told. He turned somersets on the carpet, sometimes very fast, again very slowly, even pausing while standing on his head; he sprang over the top of a book or newspaper one was reading; he snatched away eye-glasses; he made droll little leaps about a foot high, with a coquettish toss of the head and fling of the arms, and often spent a long time in thus jumping about on the floor. Above all things he liked to leap. It was not uncommon for him to spring square into one's face, sometimes grasping a nose in one hand, and an ear in the other, but occasionally embracing the face with all fours, hands on both sides of the forehead, and feet each side of the cheek. He stopped but a second; his friend was merely a station on his way to the mantel; but it was a great surprise, and though it lasted but a moment, one felt as if a tornado had passed over.

VI

KOKO'S FRIENDLINESS.

UNLIKE most beasts, this little fellow had a great liking for strangers, and frequently took violent fancies, in which case it was quite impossible to keep him away from the object of his affections. Some people liked it, but others did not : and when one young lady was actually afraid of him, he appreciated her feeling, and not only resented it by angry barking grunts, but contrived again and again to surprise her, by stealing up behind her chair and suddenly pouncing upon her. Of course she shrieked, and he squealed and grunted and ran out his tongue at her. With his friends he was troublesomely affectionate, insisting on being held on lap, arm, or shoulder, and following them from room to room, in a long, droll gallop on the floor, or by jumping from chair to table, and sometimes to their backs as they passed.

Perhaps the most amusing entertainment was his attention to a certain grave professor who spent an evening with us.

The professor was interested in animals, and as pleased to see him as was Koko himself when he found a willing victim. He began by licking the hands of his new friend, and then planted himself on the shoulder and settled to work. First he washed the face of the gentleman, holding on to the nose or laying his droll little paw flat on forehead or cheek, or grasping irreverently the full dignified beard. The face finished, greatly to the professor's delight, he began on the head. Now the professor's hair was rather thin, very neatly parted in the middle, and brushed down each side. Koko's method of treatment was peculiar; it was to scrape against the grain with his singular front teeth as he did in his own toilet.

At it he went, literally tooth and nail, and in a few minutes the professor's locks stood up as if he had been electrified, not a hair in its place. The victim sat like a martyr, closing his eyes when Koko laid a paw on them to keep his balance, and saying continually, " What a nice little fellow he is! What a dear little pet! The nicest I ever saw ! " and so on.

For half an hour or more this show went on, both having a most luxurious time, while I wished that some of the professor's many admirers who stood in awe of him could see him at the moment. He was not only a man of profound learning, but a bachelor of very particular ways. One of the family suddenly brought a small mirror and held it before his face. What a look came over him as he saw his head! He laughed long and heartily, but I observed that after he had retired and put his hair in order he did not allow the "nice little fellow" to disarrange it again, though he was just as much pleased with him.

The good-will of a captive is pleasant to have, and indeed necessary if one would know its ways ; but Koko, as I said, was too affectionate. His chosen seat was the top of one's head, but since he was never allowed to occupy that for more than an instant, he contented himself with the next desirable, namely, the shoulder of some one he liked. There he sat and dressed his fur, now and then giving a sudden lick on the cheek or ear of his victim, intended for a delicate attention, perhaps a kiss, sometimes varying this by absent-mindedly snatching a handful of the hair so near him. These marks of his devotion being not very welcome, he was forced to take a seat not quite so near the face. Next in order was an arm, on which he sat by the hour, licking the wrist as long as one could endure it, and scraping it with a push of his queer lower teeth. On somebody he was determined to be.

Almost every sound Koko uttered was like the voice of a pig. Going about the room contentedly, he constantly made a low sound like

KOKO AS HAIRDRESSER

"oof!" or "woof!" When anxious to get out of his cage the grunt was double, like the drawing in and blowing out of the breath in the same tone. His bark even was of a piggish quality. When angry or hurt, he gave a squeal and grunt together, impossible to describe; and if rubbed and caressed, he showed his pleasure by a loud, rough purr. His cry of loneliness was truly piteous; I heard it occasionally through the register. It was a sobbing, dismal sound, sometimes half a howl, sometimes with a retching quality. In uttering this he opened a small round hole of a quarter-inch diameter, in the front of his very flexible lips. If this cry is common with his tribe in the wilds of Madagascar, I do not wonder that the people are superstitious about them, and call them "spectres." No lament can be imagined more weird and heart-rending. At first, when I heard my pet cry thus, I ran hastily downstairs, thinking something dreadful had happened; but the instant his eye fell upon me, the rogue changed his wails into the grunt of recognition, and a demand to be let out.

VII

THE END OF KOKO.

AFTER five hours of revels that kept his audience in shrieks of laughter, or in terror for his life, the time came for Koko to go to bed. He was never willing; on the contrary he was determined to stay out. On this one point he never had his desire, but catching him required always a little stratagem. The cage he was careful never to enter without leaving a leg hanging out; capturing by the chase was not to be thought of, so nimble, so quick was he in movement, and so mighty in leaps; slippery and elusive was his fur to hold; there was but one way. It was for his best friend to wait patiently till he was quiet on her lap, in exactly the right position so that there should not be any chance of failure, then bring two hands down upon him suddenly and firmly, and carry him to his cage. When the hands of his friend came upon him in this way, he submitted as to fate; but if any one else tried it, he rebelled, wriggled, struggled, bit, and usually got away.

It was curious to see him prepare for the night. His bed was in a round wooden box, fast-

ened upon the side of his cage, lined and covered
with blankets. Sometimes he lay on his back,
his head hanging out upside down, and two legs
sticking out at awkward angles ; occasionally his
arms were thrown over his head, and his hands
clung to the edge of the box. But usually, after
a long preparation of fur-dressing, he placed his
head on the bottom of the box, face down, and
then disposed his body around it, wriggling and
twisting and turning till he was satisfied, when
he was seen lying on his side, his head not under
him as would be expected, and his tail curled
neatly around. Sometimes, after long and elabo-
rate arrangement, when one would not expect him
to move before morning, he suddenly started up
and came out as bright and lively as if he never
dreamed of going to sleep. But more often,
when he had thus composed himself, the heavy
blanket was dropped before his door, the lights
were turned out, and he was left for the night.

The society of Koko was entertaining through
the winter and spring, but when the weather
grew warm, a heat-loving little beast who insisted on lying full length on one's shoulder, or
clasping an arm with four very woolly limbs,
was not to be endured. So he was packed off
to the Philadelphia Zoölogical Gardens, due
arrangements having been made for his comfort.
There his playful ways and amiable disposition

made him at once a favorite, and he was put
with the chimpanzee so long a resident of the
Garden, in a cage twelve feet or more square.
Of course the two animals were closely watched
to see if they would be friends.

When the great lazy ape observed her small
cage-mate, she first honored him with a good
stare, and then reached out her long arm to take
hold of him. This, however, was a stranger
Koko did not care to spring upon; he slipped
away. She moved a step or two, he retreated
slowly, but careful to be just out of her reach.
She followed him around the cage; still he eluded
her. The chase began to be interesting. He
took refuge on certain beams put across for her
use; she followed. Higher and farther he
climbed, she close at his heels, till he reached the
highest and the farthest corner whence was no
retreat. On she came, sure now of her game,
as were also the spectators, who looked on with
deep interest to see if she would be amiable.
Suddenly, just as she stretched out her hands to
seize him, he rose over her head with a bound,
and came through the air to the other side of the
cage, almost as though he had wings. Never
was an audience more surprised.

Although Koko would not allow the chimpanzee to catch him, the two soon became excel-
lent friends, and furnished great amusement for

visitors for a year, perhaps longer. The strong bond between them seemed to be, that his greatest happiness was to scrape and dress and work over hair, and her greatest happiness was to have it done.

Passing through Philadelphia a year afterward, I stopped at the Gardens to see how my little pet fared with a stranger of his own kind, who had lately been added to the happy family in the chimpanzee cage. Sure enough! there I saw two lemurs, one sitting over behind a box nearly hidden, and the other frolicking in the front. Was this Koko? He bounded about in the same way, though with not so much spirit, and he had the same vacant stare at something back of his audience, never meeting one's eyes. It was exactly like him, perhaps a little grown. After a while he came near the chimpanzee, who lay quietly on the straw as if she were ill. Seeing him approach, she put out her hand to push him away, and in fact, though he made several attempts to get close to her, she would not allow it. But now the other lemur came from behind the box, a perfect copy of the first, only perhaps a little smaller. With the assurance of established custom he ran up to the chimpanzee and began to dress her hair. She closed her eyes in contentment, and I knew this was Koko.

IV.

THE MARMOSET.

I. MEPHISTOPHELES.

THE most unique ornament that ever adorned my mantel was a comical looking little fellow, who usurped the place of bric-à-brac in my house, — porcelain and pottery, curios and carvings were all swept out of sight, and the whole length and breadth given up to an eight-inch fellow, whose "tricks and manners" were household entertainment for months.

He might generally be seen sitting inside a low box, covered with a blanket shawl, his funny little hands with fingers wide spread resting on the edge, and quaint face peering out from under the gray shawl to see that nothing happened without his knowledge. With his coal-black complexion, and long silvery hair lying smoothly back over the top of his head, as though held by a round comb, he exactly resembled a very black old lady, with a very white cap and dirty white gloves.

Nor was the illusion quite destroyed when, in a moment, something interested him, and he gracefully lifted the shawl and stepped out in full sight. The rather long fur of the arms and under parts gave him the appearance of wearing a white, long-sleeved apron over his reddish-brown dress.

The home, the eating and sleeping place of the little beast, whose name was *Midas Pinche*, was on the mantel, but he had by way of change, and to afford a chance for outings, a highway to the floor in the shape of an old-fashioned easy chair. The piece of carving at the top was his favorite seat, from which he looked upon the strange human world he found about him. Descending to the arms, he had on the left a cushioned seat before the bright grate fire, and on the right a somewhat distant outlook into the sunshine through the windows. On rare occasions he went to the floor, and made efforts to climb the slender leg of an upright piano, across the fireplace from his chair. A laughable figure he was too, his white arms clasping the leg, and his queer face turned toward me to see if I intended to allow it. So far and no farther, was his range, defined for him by the length of a cord attached to a belt around the body, and very seldom, indeed, did he attempt to take a step beyond his limits.

On one occasion, there being no fire, a centre-table was moved nearer than usual to the mantel,

and quite unexpectedly, as I sat beside it reading, the monkey came with a bound upon it. I
was alone and he was not startled, so he proceeded to make careful study of everything
upon it — books, papers, and lastly a small
Japanese tray on which was fastened a bronze
frog about half an inch long. After some
examination of this creature, he cautiously approached and pounced upon it with both hands,
showing that he was familiar with the business
of catching insects. While he was busily lifting the corners of newspapers, as if looking for
something he had lost, I happened to turn suddenly, when he made one tremendous bound and
landed on the mantel, four feet away. I don't
know which of us was the most startled.

From his mantel or the top of his chair, our
South American guest — as I said — looked on
at the life about him, and expressed his views of
the same, with great freedom. He knew every
one of the family, and had his opinion of them
too, and he considered the presence of a stranger
entirely uncalled for, and not to be tolerated.

He watched one who came in very closely,
with a grave air of suspicion, and generally
ended his scrutiny by a vehement harangue,
which although in his native tongue, and un-
translatable by us, left no doubt of his meaning.
His manner at the time was most droll. He

turned his head over on one side in a sentimental attitude, though his feelings were far from sentimental, and began a low chattering, in a sweet birdlike tone, which rapidly became louder, having notes higher and lower, longer and shorter, and passages trilled and slurred, with mouth sometimes contracted to a small round opening. It was a truly musical performance, surprising indeed from an animal.

During the delivery of this song — as I must call it — he turned his head from side to side, in the manner of a professional singer, and lastly gave a bewitching close to the whole, by a whimsical little jerk of head and body, first one side, then the other, as if trying to " show off." Sometimes this jerking movement went so far as to become " weaving," throwing his whole body on one side and bringing his hands to the mantel, then doing the same on the other side. This he kept up for several minutes, his venerable looking face, with its eager expression and large dark eyes, swinging through an arc of perhaps six inches each time. Now and then he delivered this tirade to a mischievous youth in the family, who was prone to trifle with his dignity, by seizing his temptingly long tail, or peeping under the cover after he was curled up for a nap. The mere glance of this tormentor he hotly resented. In fact he much disliked to have any one look at him ; it seemed to give him a nervous shock. Sometimes, too, he thus reproved even his mistress, when she offended him by putting on eyeglasses, or a bonnet.

From certain performances of his own, and from the unnatural actions of a dog before he came to me, the little fellow had established the reputation of being " queer " and received the extraordinary name of Mephistopheles. The dog — a very intelligent spaniel — looked upon him with peculiar suspicion and disfavor. He plainly longed to shake the life out of him, as he did with a rat, but his master not allowing this, he restrained himself, at the same time declining to make friends with him, as he had with other pets in the household. He treated the marmoset always with the same reserve, and at last refused even to go into the room where he was kept, although it was his master's studio, and had been his favorite retreat. He would stand at the door and whine. and cry, and wag⁻ his tail, to show his friend that he did not lack affection for him ; but over the threshold he would not step.

II

AT BEDTIME.

Not a movement or sound in the house escaped the notice and the comments of the marmoset. A glimpse of his own reflection in the polished marble, or the glass of the book-case, always set his head twitching, a strange, quick jerking motion, that seemed to be involuntary. When a hand glass was placed on his mantel, he twitched as he caught sight of himself in the beveled edge, but when he came into full view he showed no curiosity about the marmoset before him, but an absorbing interest in the room " through the looking-glass," at which he stared so long as the glass stood there.

No elderly maiden with notions was ever more " set " against change than the monkey on the mantel. A gentleman putting his feet upon a chair he considered highly improper, and spoke his mind at once, in a sharp, though musical chatter. On one occasion of sudden company, where the youth of teasing ways had to sleep in the room, he was so excited and annoyed by his presence that he positively could not go to sleep. Drowsiness overcoming him, he went into his box and made preparations for the night ; then at the last moment he cautiously lifted his blanket with one hand, to see if the intruder were still there, and seeing him, popped out like a Jack-in-a-box, to remonstrate and scold, and demand, in his way, that things be restored to their usual order. He took great offense at any change in my dress, and if it were marked, as from a black to a white dress, he utterly refused to take his food from my hand, but chattered and " weaved " at me across the room.

A striking peculiarity of the odd little beast was his refusing to become familiar with us. After he had been in the family room for about four months, and taken his food from our hands, he was still scared out of his wits if we attempted to touch him. I never before had beast or bird who did not after a while cease to be suspicious, so that, while they might not allow liberties, they were not afraid. But that strange fellow, so long with us, persisted in regarding us as enemies, and resented our slightest touch, with screams that were truly appalling in one of his size. I attempted once to give him a treat by carrying his box, with him in it, to the window, so that he could look out. At my first movement he shrieked with terror, as if I were murdering him. He could not have made a greater outcry if I had actually attempted his life.

Bates, in his "Naturalist on the Amazon," speaks of the same behavior in the relatives of my pet in South America. He says that so long as the *Midas Ursula* is in any way confined, it refuses to be familiar, but when allowed the freedom of the house, it becomes exceedingly tame.

Never was a four-handed creature more inquisitive than my marmoset, and his attitudes were curiously human as he daintily lifted one corner of a cloth or paper, and leaned far over to peer beneath it. He was suspicious of a mystery concealed under the towel I spread over the cold marble for him, and he seemed to expect that a terrific bugaboo would some day appear through the door that looked into the dark hall.

Unlike the common marmoset, which destroys everything it touches, he was naturally gentle. A white moth, which was once given him to eat, he took in his dainty fingers, examined it closely on all sides, and then let it go without hurting it in the least.

During the summer and early fall the marmoset had perfectly regular habits of sleeping. At five o'clock he retired to his bed, in the blanket-lined box. But although so "early to bed" the little sleepy head did not carry out the old proverb, for not before eleven in the morning did he condescend to rise. As the weather grew cold he stayed longer and longer in his warm nest, and after he found that lights made the room warm in the evening, he grew more and more late in going to bed, till November, when he never left us until about eleven o'clock, though he still rose about eleven. He took many long naps during the afternoon, and I believe if it had been cold enough he would have hibernated.

He was a wise little beastie, too ; he discovered after a while that it was warmer to crawl under the shawl itself, outside of, and close against the box, and so for a month or more he did not occupy his old quarters. Still he would not allow the box to be removed; he might not choose to use it, but he knew it was his, and he wanted it in its old place, where he could climb over it on his way to bed.

So long as he slept in the box it was comical to watch his retiring. Beside the box he always stood a few moments upright, which was easy for him to do, raised with one hand the blanket cover, leaned over and peered in, with a comical air of looking under the bed for a burglar. Finding things all right, he glanced around the room to see that all was safe there, then dived under the blanket, resting his feet (or hinder hands) on the edge of the box a moment, while his long tail curled itself up from the tip like a watchspring, and passed in before the body, when he instantly dropped under the cover. Often as we saw the performance, it never ceased to be extremely funny.

Once inside his bed with his cherished tail, he sat down with this member standing up before him, on edge, like a wheel, thrust his head between his knees beside it, and thus arranged in a compact bundle, almost as round as a ball, he slept, the top of his head on the floor, and his nose buried in his fur. How he could breathe was a problem. Soon after he was in bed we heard the most tender, sweet, and bird-like calls and cries which were really touching, for they seemed like lamentations for his mates or dreams of home.

When getting-up time came, the little fellow uncoiled himself ; we heard gentle stirrings, and a low, single chirp, — a true bird note. In a moment a corner of the shawl was lifted, a wide-awake black face with its crown of silver hair appeared, looking, as I said, comically like a black old lady with a white nightcap. The next instant out stepped the marmoset, stretching himself, and showing us how long and thin he really was. His usual position was sitting up like a squirrel, when he looked round and plump enough.

III

LIFE ON THE MANTEL.

As soon as the marmoset was up he hurried to his favorite seat, the top of the armchair, and immediately called for his breakfast, with his usual cry, a sort of long drawn out " e-e-e" in a musical voice, each note a tone higher and a little longer than the one before it.

At once his breakfast was brought. If it happened to be bread and milk, he first drank the milk, and then ate the soaked bread. If it were grapes, he poked one into his mouth out of sight, even though it were a big Concord grape, chewed till the pulp came out, then took the skin in one hand and the pulp in the other, and licked off the juice, rejecting what was left. A pear, if soft, he took in both arms and scooped out the inside with his tongue, leaving the skin an empty cup, thin as the finest of china. A slice of pear or apple he held in both hands and bit, when he looked like a small black boy with a slice of watermelon.

The diet of my pet was at first bananas alone, and his pranks with this food were intolerable on a mantel, however they might do

in his native woods. He took a thin slice in his
hands, bit off twice as much as he could manage, and at every movement of the jaws, thrust
the mouthful out on his tongue. After two or
three chews he gave his head a quick toss, that
flung the surplus off on to carpet and wall and
furniture, which was soon ornamented with
small wads of sticky banana hard to remove.
After enduring it some time I began to experi-
ment, and found that the naughty rogue would
eat many things, and then banana was no longer
on his bill of fare.

The *Midas pinche* was perhaps eight inches
long in body, with a tail of sixteen or eighteen
inches; he would not let us come near enough to
measure it. As already mentioned, his face was
coal-black, while the long silky hair that hung
down on his shoulders was a beautiful silver-
white. He had also a curious line of long white
hairs on his bare face, starting from near the
corner of the eyes and falling off each side like
a fashionable mustache, and his nearly white
eyebrows met in the middle and were quite
heavy.

All of this gave him a truly venerable look,
aside from the fact that his face itself looked as
if he might be a hundred years old. His ears
were bare of hair, very human looking, and
ended in a little point at the top.

Unlike most of the monkey tribe, he would look one squarely in the eye, and not flinch. On the hands the fingers were long and slim, but there was no opposable thumb, while on the feet — as we naturally called the hinder pair of hands — there was a decided thumb. All his fingers had claws and not nails.

This funny tenant of my mantel never washed face or hands, and paid no attention to his coat, with one exception, — his tail. This apparently useless appendage, twice as long as he was, which usually hung straight down, or stood straight out, gave him much concern, and was evidently the one point on which he prided himself. To dress it, he brought it up before him, held it with one hand and combed it violently with the claws of the other, — the wrong way of the fur. When he got too far up in his operations to reach while sitting (for the tail towered above his head like a flagpole), he rose to his feet, and stretched up in a ludicrous way. It never seemed to occur to him to draw the prim tail down. In fact he acted as if it belonged to somebody else. He often sat and held it up before his face, contemplating it with an air of grave interest and curiosity, as who should say " What is this that I see before me?"

In fright, the beautiful silky hair of his head rose so much as to change his expression, while

THE MARMOSETS

that on the tail stood out all around; and in anger the member itself was "swished" like that of an angry cat. In fact, although he was afraid of people, when he was really cornered he became savage, and showed that, notwithstanding he was a pet and lived on a mantel, he might be a very unpleasant beast to manage, a genuine wild monkey.

As the weather grew colder in the fall, the little monkey hardly came out at all, from his warm corner under the blanket. One day I bethought me of trying to comfort him with a footstove. I got a flat stone three or four inches square and an inch thick. This I put on the kitchen range till it was very warm, then wrapped it in flannel and laid it in the path of the shivering little fellow. When he came out to breakfast and stepped on it, he instantly stopped, and nothing would induce him to leave it till it grew cold. After that I kept it heated for him all the time he was awake, and he hugged it as a freezing person will hug a stove.

But as the weeks went on he grew more and more sleepy and dull, so that he was no longer amusing, and I knew he would not brighten up till summer came. So I moved his quarters to another place, and never again tried to keep a monkey on the mantel.

IV

RAVINI AND RAVENINI: THE SMALLEST MONKEYS IN THE WORLD.

THE marmoset that lived on my mantel gave me much pleasure, but none of these little fellows are half so charming when they are confined in any way as when they are free.

The house of a friend living not far from me was, a few years ago, the home of two of the smallest monkeys in the world.

They were brought from Brazil by the son of the house, and his mother was horrified when he told her what he had done.

"Monkeys, of all things! and two of them at that!" she cried. "What on earth can I do with them?"

"But mother" — he began, "they 're not very big."

"They 're so mischievous! They 'll be up to all sorts of pranks, and I shall not be able to sleep nights," went on the mistress of the beautiful home, unused to pets.

For answer, the tall son drew one hand out of his pocket, held it toward her, and opened it.

There sat a marmoset, the smallest of the monkey family, not nearly so big as his fist.

Before his mother could speak, he held the other hand out, and there sat another monkey, almost the twin brother of the first.

"Oh, what cunning little creatures! Are these your monkeys?" burst out the mother in changed tones, and coming nearer. "The dear little fellows! do let me take them!" and she put out her hand.

The smaller of the two accepted the offer, sprang into her hand, and ran up her arm to her shoulder, where he sat down to a close study of the lace in her neck. But the other one greeted her with a sharp chattering, and hastened to hide himself at the back of the neck of his master, cuddled down inside his collar. No more coaxing was needed. The little strangers won the heart of the whole household, and before night every one was as fond of them as their owner. They were the Pigmy Marmoset, four inches tall when standing up, and so light one could sit on the edge of a china teacup and not upset it.

Nothing was ever more funny to look at than a rough-and-tumble fight between these two little beasts, when they would wrestle violently together, throw each other down freely, scold and chatter, with plenty of room to spare — all in the palm of a lady's hand.

A comical performance, too, was their hunt for sugarplums, of which they were very fond. They soon learned by experience that the desired bits of candy were sometimes to be found inside the mouth of the lady who "did n't want any monkeys" before she saw them. All she had to do was to open her mouth wide, when there was a rush and a scramble to be first to explore that curious candy-box.

The first one who got there stood on her hand or her shoulder, or any convenient place, rested his funny little hands on her teeth, and thrust his little round head out of sight in her mouth, turning it this way and that till he spied the tidbit, when he snatched it out and retired to a safe place to eat it. This might be on top of her head, or inside her neck ruche against her neck, which warm nest he was very fond of. This seems like a strange performance, and if I had not seen it many times, I should hesitate about telling it.

If it was the bigger of the two who captured the dainty, he ate it in peace, for he was not so good-tempered as his companion, and never allowed interference with his comfort.

But if the smaller one proved the more nimble and secured the prize, he had to run and hide, and sometimes fight for his rights. Even then he did not always secure them, for his brother was down upon him like a flash, with a sharp chatter, and often snatched the candy away.

The notion they got by this performance was that an open mouth was an invitation to hunt for sugarplums, and this made a funny scene one day. A gentleman visitor was talking and laughing in the room, when one of the marmosets noticed that his mouth was unusually large, and frequently opened in a most tempting way. He quietly stole up on to the man's knee, then, not being noticed, he ran up his arm, and at last from the top of his shoulder gazed longingly into the attractive opening.

No friendly hand, however, was held up to the chin for him to stand upon, and it was some distance from the shoulder. He stood and looked earnestly, while all the room full—except the gentleman himself—were watching him.

At last the poor little fellow grew desperate, and when a hearty laugh opened wider than usual the tantalizing candy-box, as he thought it, he took one flying leap, landed somewhere (it was done so quickly that no one could say where), and head and shoulders disappeared within the tempting cavity.

There was a cry of horror from the spectators, who had not imagined that he would go so far, a yell of dismay from the victim, a jerk of the tail from his master, and the poor little beastie learned roughly, that not everybody kept candy in the mouth, or enjoyed having a monkey, however small and dainty, explore it.

I said the larger of the two was somewhat ill-tempered, but it was only during the first few days that he appeared so, and there proved to be a very good reason for it.

When the little creatures were brought on board the ship in Brazil, they were not caged, but held by cords tied around the body, and thus they were kept on the ship. But their kind mistress did not want them confined, so she took her scissors to remove the cord. In the case of the larger monkey, she found it so tight that it was with great difficulty that she could get the scissors under to cut it.

The poor little fellow must have suffered greatly. He chattered and fought her, but the moment it was cut he was relieved, and before long he was as amiable as his brother marmoset. That kind deed attached him deeply to his mistress, and he displayed his affection by wanting to kiss her all the time.

V.

A VISIT TO THE MARMOSETS.

THE smallest monkeys in the world were a pretty gray color, and had on each side of their faces tufts of dark hair, which were brushed back over their ears. Their tails, three times as long as their bodies, were covered to the tip with hair, in gray and black rings.

Nothing could be prettier than their tiny round faces, with the bright, intelligent black eyes, and mouth, when wide open, about as big as a sugarplum. On their heads was a growth of darker hair, which started from the forehead like that on a human head, and gave them a curious resemblance to us.

As soon as they were received into the family, names were found for them, which I shall spell as they sounded. The larger was Ravini Racker, and the smaller was Ravenini Hipticoro, the *i* pronounced like *e*. The name in the books is *Hapale pygmæ*, and it is neither so long nor so hard to remember as the home names.

The first time I saw the marmosets I was shown into the room where they were alone, cuddled down in a soft blanket shawl on a sofa.

I went up to look at them and speak to them; but at the first word they turned on me as fiercely as though they had been four feet tall instead of four inches. They chattered and scolded in a voice like a canary bird's whisper, and finding that I was not frightened, and really meant to come nearer, they scrambled out of their warm corner, scampered across the room, caught at a lace curtain, and ran like two gray streaks to the top.

Arrived at the safe elevation of the cornice, they calmly sat down and proceeded to examine me, turning their quaint little faces on one side and then the other in a very saucy-looking manner. But I wanted to see them nearer, and I had come provided with attractions, in the shape of sugarplums. I selected a bright-red one and held it in my hand where their sharp eyes would see it, and placed myself so that the lace-curtain highway touched my shoulder.

They noticed the bait instantly, and after some chattering, and many sharp looks at me, the larger of the two decided to risk it. He ran down the curtain to my shoulder, turned a moment toward my face with a sharp remark, as if to say, " I trust myself with you, but you may be sure I can take care of myself. so you need n't presume; " then ran down my arm, snatched the candy, and stuffed it into his mouth. He intended to return to the cornice to devour it at his leisure, but I had quietly stepped back from the curtain, so far that he did not care to jump, and as I did not attempt to touch him, he decided to make the best of it.

He returned to my hand, sat up and proceeded to dispose of his prize, while I in turn studied him. He never took his alert eyes off my face, and after he had eaten the candy he started on a tour of discovery. The material of my dress was scrutinized, a falling lock of hair examined, perhaps with the idea of adding it to his bed, and the flowers of my bonnet tasted and rejected as hollow mockeries.

The treasure which rewarded his search, however, was a rose in my dress. This he took out of its place, and went on to demolish. Each petal he pulled off deliberately, dropped it to the carpet, and looked over after it as it fell. He nibbled the green leaves and at last ran off with the bare stem as a trophy.

Then he began to call to his mate, who all this time was performing droll gymnastic feats on a picture cord. He replied with a sharp little whistle. My little visitor ran quickly down my dress, across the floor, up the curtain, across the cornice, and down the picture cord, and seated himself on top of the small picture frame beside his friend.

Then in a musical chatter, low, but very sweet, like a soft canary-song, with trills and silvery calls, he told him, no doubt, all about his thrilling adventure, — his daring capture of the sugar-plum; his investigation of the sham flowers which made so brave a show; the storming and utter destruction of the rosebud.

To all of this the little fellow on the picture frame listened and replied with interest, and then both sat still and looked at me, with funny little heads held over one side, — the most comical pair I ever saw.

Among other things of interest that their master had brought from Brazil was a box of the beautiful beetles which are found in that country. When he came into the room to see me, he brought out the box for me to look at. They were of all sizes, from a tiny creature of sapphire blue a quarter of an inch long, to a monster of three inches with horns ferocious to behold. We were much interested in these, and were soon bending over them, entirely forgetting the two marmosets on the picture frame.

But the elder, Ravini, was interested also. In those beautiful strangers in the box he recognized familiar objects, and remembered well that under each brilliant coat was a delicious morsel of meat. We were all absorbed, and again the little beast set out on a dangerous expedition.

The first we saw of him, he dropped down among those beetles with a bounce, snatched one or two, galloped across the floor, and scrambled to the top of the lace curtain like a flash. His master sprang after him, and coaxed and threatened in vain. The saucy marmoset chattered back, and calmly devoured them to the last eatable morsel, leaving nothing but the gorgeous wing-cases, which dropped to the floor.

Observing that the sharp little eyes were again fixed on the box, and that the two he had captured had merely whetted his appetite for costly beetles, his master covered up the box and decided to exhibit his treasures in another room.

At another time the marmoset saw something that reminded him of home, probably. At any rate he resolved to help himself, and did. His master had brought a large collection of postage stamps, to give to his friends. While sorting and arranging them one day on the table he was suddenly surprised by a visit from Master Ravini, who alighted in the middle of his stamps, snatched both hands full, and decamped so quickly that he could not be caught by anybody too heavy to follow him up his ladder of lace. Regrets were useless ; he could not be made to give them up, and the annoyed stamp-collector had to stand and see him tear them to bits too small to be repaired.

VI

MONKEY TRICKS.

So little were the two marmosets that a mantel with its various ornaments was a big field for discoveries. For my entertainment, Ravini was placed on a mantel. First he went for a clock that had a large and attractive pendulum swinging outside. The marmoset accepted this as a swing. He sprang on, and clung tightly while the pendulum carried him back and forth. This was great fun, and I don't know how long he would have kept it up, but he happened to notice a cologne bottle.

This new curiosity must be examined, so he left his swing and pounced upon that, running or climbing quickly to the top. He seemed to be familiar with bottles, for he pulled out the stopper at once, and tried to reach the fluid within, probably hoping it was good to drink. First he put his face to the neck and peered sharply in, then he smelled as hard as he could, and finally he thrust his arm in and tried to reach down. But the cologne was low, and he could not get at it. At last he consoled himself by seating himself on top, in place of the stopper.

It was an ample seat for him, and a droll figure he made perched up there.

Then a common lead-pencil was held out for him to perch on. He readily accepted it, and used it for various gymnastics. He hung from it, head down, turned somersets on it, and " skinned the cat " (his master said). Then Ravenini was invited to join him on the pencil, and they together performed the oddest and funniest feats one can imagine.

The marmosets refused to live in a big cage which was bought for them, and of course the freedom in a large house, of creatures so small and so curious, made great care of doors and windows necessary. If one were open three minutes the little rogues would slip out and start on a tour of the house.

One day their master came into the room where they were kept, and found the door open. The marmosets were gone ! He looked in their shawl, on the sofa, behind the picture frames, on top of the cornices : no monkeys to be found. He then called for help, and the house was searched from cellar to attic, — no small undertaking when one remembers that one of them could hide in a teacup.

Still no little beasties to be found, and that house went into mourning. After an hour or two the house mother came home, and removing her street shoes, thrust one into the shoe-bag which hung on the closet door. It did not go in far, and instantly there was a scramble and two little heads appeared at the edge of the bag, scolding furiously at her for daring to disturb their nap.

Although these little fellows are the smallest of monkeys, they are by no means stupid. Neither are they alike in temperament or taste. One of them, for example, preferred boiled onion to any other food, while the other set his affections on baked apples. Ravenini was an affectionate little fellow, and liked to cuddle down into a warm hand for a nap. He also was more timid with strangers, and not so greedy as his elder, nor so eager for adventures. Both were very quick to make up their minds whom they liked and whom they disliked among people. They agreed in avoiding children altogether. Some grown people, too, they would not go near; while others, no more attractive to human observers, they would accept at once as friends, and run over them without fear.

They were very fond of playing, both with each other and with people. Ravini, indeed, played "bo-peep" as well as anybody. He would run down the lace curtain till below the lambrequin, which hung two or three feet from the cornice, and wait there for some one to start for him. The instant one accepted his challenge and started, he scampered to the top of the cornice, peeped over, and chattered out his "bo-peep." If his playmate then walked back a few steps he would come down again, and do it all over. This game he would keep up till he tired out everybody.

A curious thing was their manner of eating loaf sugar. They doted on this luxury, and when one of them received the treasure, he at once retired to a safe place, holding it in his arms with great care. Then he seated himself to enjoy his feast. He used only his tongue, licking it in one spot till he dug out a little round hole. When he had eaten all he wanted, there would be left in the square lump a little cup-shaped cavity about big enough to hold a small pea.

Animals that are kept in the house, as all pet-keepers know, must have the care that we give to people who live in a house, or they will be very unpleasant house-mates. These little fellows were bathed and thoroughly brushed every day by their mistress. At first they rebelled at the bathing, but after a few trials they came to like it, and the brushing that followed kept their fur coats in the most beautiful condition.

But life in our climate is hard on the natives of the tropics. One of the pets died before the next winter. The survivor was greatly grieved and dreadfully lonely. He was not happy, nor even contented a moment, away from his mistress. So she procured a little basket, one of the kind made to hold a ball of knitting-yarn. This she furnished with warm wraps, and here she established the desolate monkey. Then she hung the whole affair — monkey and all — to her belt, and carried it with her wherever she went.

He was thus made as happy as possible; but the climate was not favorable to health, and at the end of a year, or possibly a little more, he too drooped, and slept his last sleep in his little basket.

VII.

ANOTHER PAIR OF MARMOSETS.

AFTER the death of the smallest monkeys in the world, I was able for a year or two to look out of my window and see another pair of marmosets, who lived in a big cage at a neighbor's, and were put out on a back piazza on pleasant days. They were larger than those I have told about, but they were sometimes very amusing.

People often say that marmosets are stupid. They are not so intelligent as the larger monkeys, but one reason why they appear so, is that they are shut in a cage. We all know how dull and listless even a dog will get who is always confined, and the case is worse with these little creatures, the most restless and active animals in the world.

What, indeed, could any one do, shut up in a cage with nothing on earth to amuse himself with?

The marmosets on the back piazza had great frolics among themselves. They rolled and tumbled together on the floor like two kittens; they "played tag" all over the cage, chasing each other madly, and, sometimes seizing the

playmate, they dropped in a wriggling heap on
the floor. Through all the fun I was amused to
see what good care they took of their long tails,
— twice as long as they were. During their maddest pranks the tail was held one side, and often
the only thing I could see in a squabble on the
floor was a mass of gray fur and two tails sticking up, waving frantically in the air.

Their cage was furnished with all desirable
gymnastic appliances, — two bars, a wire basket, and a hanging cord. Over and under and
around and through these, the monkeys frisked
like — well, like nothing but lively monkeys.
They hung head down, from one hand, or two;
they ran across, hanging back down from the
perch, like the pictures of the sloth; and they
turned somersets of the wildest kind. When
anything startled them, they darted into their
sleeping-box, which was fastened up under their
roof, with a round door just big enough for one
to go in. A droll performance this was, for the
instant one was in, and had jerked his long tail
in behind him, his head appeared at the door
to see what had happened in that half second.

Their floor was carpeted with newspaper, and
that gave them as much fun as it used to give
my little half-monkey. They frolicked over and
under it; they tore it to pieces and scattered
the fragments far and wide; and they in some

way made balls of it, I hardly know how. They were more tame than my little pet was, and they ate or drank from a teaspoon in the hand of their mistress.

The funniest thing, however, was to see the actions of a half-grown kitten about the cage. To her it was a constant circus, and she spent hours gazing at them. Generally she was quiet, and merely looked on at what happened; but sometimes she seemed to feel that they were having too good times, and longed to share them. On these occasions she went to the top of the cage, the coarse wire gauze making a convenient ladder, and looked down at them. Then they would come up near her and thrust out their little hands. Woe to her long tail if she let it rest on the wires; and woe also to her feet if she looked not where she stepped. The four little hands below were all ready, and four little eyes were sharp to see a chance.

But pussy was cautious. She walked carefully on the narrow board of the frame, and she lay down over the top of their sleeping-box, and they could not touch her. Then she would thrust her paws out and pat the wires, upon which the marmosets would tumble over each other in their scramble for the other side of the cage. Then she turned her face away, and they would hasten back to give her a nip if they could reach her.

The two were nearly the same size, but one had shining white ear-tufts each side of his black face, while the other had a full head of long black hair hanging down on his shoulders, making him look like an old withered-up Indian. For my own convenience, I named them Blackhead and Whitehead.

They were not always in a frolic. I sometimes saw the two sit close together, side by side, on a perch, for an hour together; not moving, and looking almost as if they were " stuffed," with two long tails hanging motionless below.

I don't believe my neighbor who owned these little fellows had half so much pleasure with them as I had.

All through one summer the marmosets lived in the cage on the back piazza, and during the winter that followed I used to see them occasionally through a window. But the next spring, when the weather got warm and the cage again appeared out of doors, a great change came to them : their cage door was set open for them to go in and out as they chose. At first they were very shy of the big world, — venturing out cautiously, and contenting themselves with climbing over the vines that shaded their piazza. But before long they extended their rambles into the yard, and finally reached the back fence, that highway through the block, with a branch running to every back door, which in the city belongs, by long custom, to the cats.

As soon as the marmosets learned the possibilities of the fence, they were happy. They could run from one end of the block to the other, and visit every kitchen in the row. And then they were very busy from morning till night, making new friends, and getting choice bits to eat in nearly every yard.

This intrusion upon their exclusive highway did not pass unnoticed by the cats, and I looked with anxiety for the fate of a marmoset when it should come in the way of pussy. I need not have worried about them, for, strange to say, the cats, one and all, gave the odd little beasties a wide berth. Though so much bigger, they seemed to be afraid of the monkeys, and ran away from them.

Sometimes a very brave cat would crouch on the fence about three feet from a marmoset, and wait, in cat fashion, to see what he would do. That did not disturb the little fellow in the least. If it was his whim to pass her, he would simply give a great leap over her head and land on the fence the other side, while the cat would tear across the nearest yard, frightened half out of her wits.

Promptly at four o'clock in the long summer

days, the little marmosets would turn toward home.   Many days I watched them crossing the lawn in hurried gallops, scrambling up the steps and into their cage, and disappearing within their sleeping - box, to be seen no more till morning.

V.

THE CHIMPANZEE.

I. MR. CROWLEY.

IF one could judge by the crowds that flocked to see him, the most interesting personage in New York in his day was Mr. Crowley, the chimpanzee. From early morning, through the long summer days, he held his levees, and to get a satisfactory look at him one was obliged to take his place in the jam, and patiently work his way step by step, as one after another retired, till he penetrated to the rail that defined the "safety point" before the cage.

The animal was fully aware of his position as entertainer to this ever-varying crowd. He was also perfectly competent for the task; in fact it was no task at all, for he delighted in it, and enjoyed the shouts and laughter as much as an actor his applause.

Sometimes, if one got into the building before the public was admitted, Crowley would come to the front, sit down and examine his visitor, exchange the compliments of the morning, that is to say, listen gravely to the remarks of his

guest, and answer by most expressive panto-
mime. Under these circumstances he appeared
gentle and friendly, and as if he might be made
companionable. He looked one steadily in the
eye, without that furtive glance that makes us
always suspect the next move of a monkey; he
observed dress and manners with an air of interest. That he had thoughts and opinions of
his own no one who studied him closely could
doubt, and the stranger often felt inclined to
offer his next of kin a friendly hand through
the bars. But when the ropes at the entrance
were taken down, and the waiting multitudes
trooped in, — men and boys, if early, women and
children at a later hour, — instantly the human
disappeared and the monkey came to the front;
the thoughtful fellow-creature became a buffoon.
He sprang from his seat, took a flying leap to
the roof, crossed it by two or three swings of his
long arms, and flung himself upon his two trapezes — which were, perhaps, six feet apart —
with a violence that would destroy anything less
strong than those inch-thick iron bars. On and
around these he performed mad capers that
made the spectator hold his breath, lest he get
his death-blow from the erratic movement of
the heavy iron swings. The ape had no misgiv-
ings; his agility was equal to the demand, and
he kept both trapezes in violent and irregular

motion, while he plunged over, under, around, through, between, before, behind, and every other possible way, all so rapidly that there appeared only a mass of swaying and tossing iron and wood, and a kaleidoscopic vision of legs and arms inextricably mixed up therewith. He soon tired of this, leaped to his spring-board, turned a somerset or two, and stood on his head, with feet on the board beside it and hands on the floor below ; then like a flash slipped around under the board, embracing it with all fours while he jounced himself up and down, bumping his back on the floor at every jolt.

This lasted but a minute. After a bounce or two across the cage and a swarming all over the bars of the front, he would suddenly come to the floor with a thump, gallop around near the walls, one hand slyly sweeping the floor, and quick as thought fling a handful of damp sawdust into the faces of his laughing audience outside. While they coughed and rubbed their eyes and brushed their clothes, he chuckled with delight, and turned somersets all around his cage, or ran around at full speed, driving his head through the dust of his floor like a plough.

Sawdust-throwing was his favorite insult. While his portrait was being painted, he resented the personal attentions of the artist, Mr. James H. Beard, by showering this material, not over the gentleman himself, but, with discriminating understanding of where it would be most annoying, upon the fresh paint of the portrait, whence it had to be picked bit by bit.

If a moment arrived when Mr. Crowley did not frantically desire to play some prank, he came to the front, made faces, and jumped up a few inches, with arms and legs held stiff and body upright, coming down on the floor again and again with a thump, as if feet and hands were made of iron. In fact his footsteps, at least during his public exhibitions, were usually of this character. Unless he was on some sly mischief bent, he went about like an iron-shod horse, galloping over the boards, though he weighed but ninety pounds. The baby in the adjoining cage — for there was a baby, Crowley's future spouse — did the same thing, so it must be a chimpanzee fashion. On the whole, Mr. Crowley irresistibly reminded one of a boy at the "showing-off" period of life; and with these fantastic tricks he kept his constantly varying jam of admirers in roars of laughter the whole day.

We had no reason to look for anything different, for after he came to New York an infant of about eight months, weighing between ten and twelve pounds, his life was passed almost entirely on the exhibition stage. At that re-

mote time in his existence Crowley was very
attractive, for a young chimpanzee is one of the
drollest of beasts, although so much like human
babies as to be almost painful to look at. All
the anthropoid apes, our next of kin, resemble
us in infancy, in a much greater degree than
in age. As years go over the head of man he
becomes wiser, and generally more amiable in
temper; while the ape, on the contrary, grows
wary, sly, and more brutal.

Mr. Crowley was in his infancy when he
came to New York. He had the advantage of a
training by refined people; consequently no bad
habits or tricks had developed. He passed
almost from his mother's arms into the family
of Mr. Smythe, United States Minister Resident at Liberia, who, with his wife, cared for
the little beast as tenderly as they could for a
child. On the passage he shared the comforts
of the cabin; at hotels his board was paid; thus
he had every attention, and reached New York
in perfect health, and showing a pleasing wil-
lingness to respond to the friendly advances of
everybody.

II

MR. CROWLEY'S TABLE MANNERS.

In the first winter of his residence in Central Park Mr. Crowley had a dangerous attack of pneumonia, during which there were daily bulletins in the papers, as though he were a public personage. The best medical advice was secured, and he was treated exactly like a child. He submitted cheerfully to poultices and remedies, and completely recovered his health, though after that, as a precautionary measure, he had with dinner his daily spoonful of cod-liver oil, which he enjoyed greatly.

Mr. Conklin attributed Crowley's perfect health and condition to the fact that he was thoroughly acclimated, and never made tender by living behind glass. On the contrary, he passed his days in a cage, twelve or fifteen feet square, open on one whole side to the air of an animal house, which had both ends wide open to the outside. He went daily back and forth, in the arms of his keeper, from this show-room to his sleeping-room in another building, uncovered and without taking cold. In the winter, it is true, when constant fires become necessary to us, he was removed to a close building; but even then he had the air of an ordinary house, with its varying temperature. His diet also was a subject of care. He was never allowed some of man's indulgences which, because they appear funny for an animal, are often given to him; tea and coffee, strong drinks, candy, meats, and many things we use were never seen on his table. Rice or oatmeal and milk, with fruit of different kinds, and sometimes boiled eggs, formed his frugal bill of fare, and his robust health bore witness to the wisdom of this course.

Susceptibility to training is one of the most attractive qualities of these great apes. It was to be regretted that Crowley's capabilities could never be known, since he was so constantly on exhibition that the necessary quiet and leisure were not obtainable. His dear five hundred friends never would consent to spare him from society long enough for an education. His " culture," therefore, was limited to the table manners that he brought with him.

These table ceremonies were a source of ever fresh interest. As the hour for his breakfast (half past ten) or for his dinner (five in the afternoon) drew near, the crowd grew more dense in front of his reception room. A table was brought in, the cloth spread, a chair placed before it, and a soup-plate of rice and milk served.

If Mr. Crowley happened to be hungry he rested from his performances, and came, like anybody else, at once to the table; but if he had rather more fruit at his early morning luncheon than usual, or if very much excited about anything, he acted precisely as does a naughty child under the circumstances, — he would not come; he pranced around the cage, jounced on the spring-board, set the trapezes in violent motion, ran up a ladder with his hands, and hung head down over the table as if he would drop and annihilate it. The keeper meanwhile scolded, threatened to "give it to Kitty," and in fact behaved exactly like an exasperated nurse in the presence of a willful youngster. When he did come, he seated himself decorously, spread his napkin over his knees, or sometimes crumpled it in his left hand, took the spoon in his right, and devoted himself to the business before him. That this was not play, but a serious matter, he fully recognized, and he conducted himself accordingly. He handled the spoon as dexterously as anybody, and readily put the napkin to its proper use when necessary, though occasionally his memory needed jogging by his keeper, who was at the moment table-waiter. "Mr. Crowley! where's your napkin?" sternly asked, never failed to bring the proper response.

The soup-plate emptied, and tipped up to

A RELAPSE INTO MONKEYISM

scrape the last drop, it was removed, and there
followed a plate of fruit, sliced, but not small
enough for mouthfuls. Here the knife and fork
came in, and Mr. Crowley was as skillful in cut-
ting pieces and thrusting them into his mouth —
always with the fork — as any person. He even
went so far in imitation of the manners he had
seen, as to pause now and then with a mouthful
held up on his fork, ready to shove in as soon
as he had made room in that very capacious
receptacle, his mouth. After fruit came a cup
of milk, which he took by the handle and drank,
and lastly the cod-liver oil, and a lick or two of
the spoon while his keeper was replacing the
cork, and so not looking.

When on his good behavior, he retired from
the table like a gentleman, and perhaps sprang
into his waiter's arms to be held while dinner
was removed by help of an assistant outside, or
mounted the table and danced a jig while his
attendant beat time for him. But if in a mischievous frame of mind, with the disappearance
of the last course he suffered a sudden relapse
into monkeyism, kicked over table, dishes, oil-
bottle, and all, and darted to the roof of his cage,
out of the reach of vengeance. Even on these
occasions, however, it needed only a command
from his keeper, of whom he was very fond, to
bring him down meekly to lay his knife and fork

properly and replace his napkin, after which
he immediately gave vent to his feelings by a
few dozen somersets, a fresh frolic with the trapezes, or a lively tattoo with his feet, while
clinging to a bar with his hands. Another custom of civilized life to which Mr. Crowley took
kindly was sleeping in a bed. When evening
came on, he was always very tired from his all-
day's performances, and glad to be carried over
to his room, where he quickly sprang into bed
and drew the blankets around him. He slept
till awakened by the light of morning, when he
called loudly for his early breakfast of fruit, and
then was ready for another day's entertainment.

One point at issue between the superintendent
and Mr. Crowley was the wearing of clothes.
The ape could not be convinced that the dress
of his human neighbors was either useful or
ornamental, while it certainly interfered with his
freedom of movement. Without his own consent
he could not be clothed, for no fabric has ever
been contrived strong enough to resist his mischievous fingers.

III.

A NAUGHTY CHIMPANZEE.

CROWLEY's worst quality was the irresistible propensity to destroy every object he could lay his hands on, including live animals. A dog or cat he would almost instantly tear to pieces; in fact, the sight of a small animal seemed to put him into a fury. A tiny monkey brought by a lady on her shoulder made him so wild that he acted like a maniac; he threw handful after handful of sawdust all over his audience; he shook the bars of his cage with suggestive violence; he put up his lips like a trumpet and cried "Hoo! hoo!" at it; he tore around the cage in a transport, and lastly he spit at it. This was one of the bad tricks he learned from ill-bred and teasing boys who visited him, and he became so expert that he could reach his mark eight feet away. During the above exhibition of temper the unfortunate little creature, a beautiful squirrel monkey six inches long, was out of its senses with fright, chattered, and fairly screamed in terror.

This lamentable destructive tendency demanded a strong guard-rail before the cage, at the length of Mr. Crowley's arm, for he was always ready to thrust out one of those long, sinewy members and snatch at hat, parasol, or anything he could reach ; once in his clutches it was lost. A Park policeman stood one day talking to him, inside the rail by virtue of his office, while Crowley sat on the floor close by the bars, absorbed in contemplation of his brand new white gloves. Very gently he pulled the tips of the fingers one after the other, quietly loosening them, till suddenly, like a flash, he snatched off the glove and bounded to the back of his cage. In vain the hapless policeman commanded and coaxed, begged and threatened. Mr. Crowley, entirely unmoved, sat calmly down to enjoy his prize. First he put it on his hand, using his teeth to help, and then held it up for the audience to see, with every finger spread, grinning with delight. But, not being able to arrange it to his satisfaction, he tore it to strings, and passed a happy fifteen minutes while reducing it to its primitive state of thread, holding one part in the bend of the thigh — the monkey's convenient pocket — while he worked on another.

On another occasion one of the Park men went inside of the rail to speak to the chimpanzee. Crowley sat quietly on the floor looking at him, and thrusting his hands out to play, as was his custom.

" Look out, there!" warned the keeper.

"Oh, Mr. Crowley knows me," was hardly out of his mouth in response, before Mr. Crowley fastened his fingers upon the lapels of his coat, one each side, and gave them such a jerk that the man was dashed violently against the bars, and the coat split down the back like so much paper.

This animal proved so attractive to the public that the Park Commissioners thought they would provide him with a playmate. An order for a young female chimpanzee was therefore sent out, and after two years of waiting a promising personage named Kitty was brought to New York. The baby, for she was but an infant, being two years old and about half the size of Crowley, was very pretty, — for an ape, — and a charmingly amiable and frolicsome little creature. Not possessed by the mania of tearing everything to bits, she could be trusted with a hammock, in which she played all sorts of amusing pranks, and a red shawl, the delight of her heart. She was introduced to Mr. Crowley by placing her in the next cage to his, separated by a close partition, in one part of which were narrow openings, hardly more than cracks, through which he could see and hear, but not touch.

His reception of her was not very gallant. He went mad with rage ; he ached to tear her to

pieces ; he shouted at her ; he pounded the partition and shook the bars ; he fairly jumped up
and down in passion.   If anything was given to
her he raised a riot ; and when his audience paid
attention to her, he behaved like a tiger out of
the jungle.   In fact he showed himself to be a
ferocious wild beast.   There is no doubt that he
would have killed her instantly had she been in
his power.

But Kitty was protected by her bars, and
gradually he grew more amiable, though with
occasional relapses into his original sentiments
that augured ill for Miss Kitty's future.   He
grew wily after a little, and made use of other
tactics to get her within reach.   He came to the
bars, coaxed and chattered, and was very sociable till she came near, when he blinded her with
a handful of sawdust.   Poor Kitty retired in dis-
gust, while Crowley scampered around his cage
in a frenzy of joy, chuckling, turning somersets,
and indulging in the maddest of frolics.

Again, he thrust his long arms outside his
cage, in front, and around into her cage, his
hand feeling about to seize whatever it might
touch.   Sometimes Kitty avoided it : sometimes
she took hold of it ; occasionally she gave it
a playful bite, upon which he jerked it back,
rushed around his floor to gather a handful of
sawdust, again put his arm through the bars,

and flung it at her. Hate her as he might, he could not help being interested ; if any sound came from her side of the wall, he hurried to the opening and glued his ear or his eye to the crack, as an eavesdropper to a keyhole.

One day each of them had a stick to play with. Kitty amused herself biting hers to a point, pressing it into a hole too small to admit it, until it was reduced in size, and breaking it off, then biting it again, and repeating the operation, apparently liking the noise it made. Crowley used his stick to annoy her ; he pushed it between the bars and tried to reach her with it. She would take hold of it, when he jerked it away, and was so pleased that he chuckled and grinned most unpleasantly. After tormenting her a long time, he grew careless, and she snatched it out of his hand. Then his fury was terrible to see ; he raged round like a demon, pelted her with showers of sawdust, and became so outrageous that one of the keepers took a long iron rod with a scraper on the end, and tried to discipline him. But, so far from succeeding, Mr. Crowley turned the tables on him by snatching it out of his hand, and then he had a weapon with which he might easily kill half a dozen of his packed spectators. He had the strength to do it, too ; he handled that six-foot rod as if it were a bamboo cane. There was a sort of panic

outside ; the crowd backed ; the keeper snatched
a longer iron of the same kind and kept the
enraged beast so busy defending himself that
he had not a chance to think of the power in
his hands till the rod could be dragged out.

When cold weather forced Mr. Crowley to
take refuge in a warmed room, where the usual
jam of visitors was not admitted, he missed the
excitement, and often found time heavy on his
hands.   Then he was sometimes treated to playthings.   A ball he was fond of, and he had the
important advantage of four hands to play with.
He even evolved a new and original way to play
with that very popular toy ; he lay flat on his
back and took all-fours to it.   An exceedingly
comical picture he made of himself, too.

Tenpins he enjoyed, though he refused to
set up the pins.   When his obliging friend and
servant, his keeper, set them up, he ran across
the room and rolled the ball, making very good
shots with it.

A doll that was given to him he made use of
in his peculiar fashion, first beating it soundly
with a stick, sitting on it, jumping on it, and at
last tearing it to rags.   He could blow a whistle
as well as a boy, but his supreme treat was
winding a stem - winding watch ; a " Water-
bury " was a treasure to him, for he doted on a
half hour of steady winding.

Crowley certainly understood much, if not all, that was said to him. He was grieved by reproaches and pleased by kind words, and he managed to express his emotions clearly to his friends, though he was evidently not so fluent as some of his kind have been in captivity. This may be because he had no companions, nor even neighbors, who might be supposed to understand him, and so make it worth his while to talk. Perhaps if he had become reconciled to Kitty, and on friendly and social terms with her, we might have learned the chimpanzee language. Meanwhile he was a deeply interesting subject of study, as well as the funniest fellow in New York.

VI.

THE SPIDER MONKEY.

I. GILA.

THE dearest pet I ever had, said the friend who told me this true story, was a Spider monkey of Central America. I was greatly pleased when she was given to me, for I had often lingered in my walks to look at her pranks in the place which was then her home.

The particular thing that had amused me was her fondness for horseback-riding, and the cunning way in which she managed to gratify her taste for that sport, at the expense of the pigs that were kept in the same yard. Sitting in perfect silence on the low branch of a tree, she watched her chance, and the moment a pig wandered under her hiding place, she swung herself down and pounced upon him, taking a good grip of his ears to hold on by.

The steed needed no spur. He galloped off at the top of his speed, and tore furiously around the yard, evidently not pleased to play horse, but unable to shake her off till she was tired and dismounted herself.

THE SPIDER MONKEY

Unlike most of the race, spider monkeys are fond of standing erect, and I often saw her walking about with tail held above her head, the tip curled over like the end of a letter *S*. I think I never saw anything more funny than Gila (whose name was pronounced Heela) walking down the garden path, swinging a tin pail in a business-like manner, as a workman carries a dinner-pail.

Gila was a very pretty creature. She was more than two feet tall, and weighed twelve pounds, which is quite heavy for one of her family. Her dress was a suit of long, light-yellow hair, lighter than many of her kind, and, after a few weeks' care and combing, it became beautifully soft and silky. Her face and hands were black, and her knees and feet. The skin inside her long tail was also a satiny black. With this most useful tail she could not only hang from a branch, but could hold objects. Whenever she snatched anything and ran away with it, which I regret to say was a favorite trick, she did it with her tail; though, when she sat down to look at her prize closely, she took it in her hand. Once, when not in the best of humor, she was passing the table spread for dinner, on her way to be chained up. With that too-handy tail she swept it clean, dishes and all, in one complete wreck.

Her hands were long and slim, and soft as velvet inside, but without thumbs; her thumbs were on her feet. Her eyes were of the "snapping" black sort, full of mischief, and she had a fine set of white teeth, which she sometimes used for other purposes than eating.

The common name of my pet was Black-handed Spider Monkey, but the name I gave her, which was the one she answered to, was Gila Chimpilicoco. She was intelligent, and could express her feelings as well as if she could talk. Though she had only two or three kinds of cries, she uttered them with such varying expressions that there was no need of words.

The first act of the new pet was naturally mischief. Not being expected, no place was ready for her, so I had her tied by a rope to the trunk of a small tree in full blossom, and it happened that no one noticed her for some time. She did not suffer with loneliness, however; she perfectly amused herself, if not the family. She literally stripped that tree, not only of flowers and leaves, but of twigs and small branches, and when we found her she was coolly "jouncing" herself in the branches to break them off. In a short time the whole would have been kindling wood. She screamed and chattered at us when we dragged her down, before she had finished her work to her taste.

"Now, Madame Gila," said I, as the man tied her to a post, " we'll see what you can find to do here."

She did find something; her hands were never idle. She worked at the knot of her rope till it untied, and then she proceeded to investigate the garden, her new home. Whatever green fruit she could find, she pulled off and threw down as unworthy the notice of any sensible monkey; the growing vegetables she dragged out of the ground to see what they were like; the pots of flowers she upset to examine the under side. In fact that spot of ground looked as if a hurricane had passed through it.

" Now this will never do," I said; " this Mischief must be securely fastened. I can't keep her to ruin a garden not my own."

But the secure fastening was the puzzle. It was beyond the wit of man to contrive a knot that she would not untie. At last she had to be chained, for every finger was full of " fidget " as some little people's fingers, and she had twice as many of them, besides her two thumbs. A home was also made for her that seemed safe.

The house, like all first-class houses in the city of Granada where all this happened, was built around a court which was filled with trees and flowers. Around the court, into which every room opened, was a corridor like a wide piazza, with a roof over it. Under the edge of that roof, where she could have sunshine or shade as she wished, was made Gila's home.

She soon learned many ways of civilized life, for she was a bright scholar. To eat with a fork required only one lesson, — and that 's more than can be said of our little folks, — and to take her breakfast like a lady, not "gobbling," but drinking her coffee out of a cup, was almost as soon learned. She became very fond of her morning coffee, and was wise enough to know when she might expect it. If the master of the house came into the corridor and took his early coffee, as was his custom, Gila paid no attention to him ; but the moment I appeared and seated myself for the same purpose, she began to cry and scream and tease, till for the sake of peace, she was served first, though I always insisted that she should show us some trick before I gave her the cup.

She quickly learned what I meant, and when she begged for her breakfast I had only to say, " No, no, Gila ; not till you show us a trick," when she at once stood on her head with her funny heels in the air, or, if we gave her a piece of board, she stood it up on end, climbed to the top, and sat there as long as she could keep her balance, steadying herself by her chain.

II

MORE ABOUT GILA.

Besides coffee, Gila delighted in fruits and sweets ; syrup on bread pleased her greatly, and she always made her own choice of the dishes on the table. She decided instantly what she wanted, and if it was not given to her she would accept bread or anything offered to her, but she held it without eating till she saw what became of the dish she had selected. Not until it was carried past her, on its way to the kitchen, would she make up her mind to be content with what she had.

In the middle of the day it was the custom to serve to the ladies of the family something cooling, — lemon or orangeade, or a fruit drink. Of the ladies Gila considered herself one, and the moment the servant appeared she was on the alert; no lazy swinging then, no quiet napping on her shelf ; she had her rights to look out for. By long use she had come to regard the dregs of the glasses as her share of the treat, and no miser ever watched his gold more eagerly than Gila watched the precious drink. If the servant forgot her, or the glasses were too nearly emptied, she would scream and cry.

When Gila was in her native forest, among her own people, she lived upon nuts and fruits, mangoes, bananas, oranges, and many others, but she was exceedingly willing to make experiments, and always ready to try anything she saw us eating. She soon ate exactly what the family did.

She had a curious fashion of getting a drink when it rained, that I suppose she brought from her wild home. The roof of the corridor was of tiles, shaped like cylinders cut in half. Down these little gutters the rain poured in tiny streams, and Gila would carefully hold her head so that the stream fell into her open mouth, and *not* into her eyes, and drink as much as she liked.

Like her mistress, Gila was fond of pets, and especially doted on the kitten. Once she caught her and held her tightly hugged in her arms, while chattering over her in glee; but pussy did not like it and cried pitifully. Nothing would tempt the too loving monkey to give her up, and every one had so much respect for Gila's teeth that they hesitated to try force. She petted and caressed her, examined her fur, and looked inside her ears, all the time chattering and having the most delightful time. Poor puss! sometimes she was held by one leg, and sometimes by a grip on her fur; sometimes her head was up and sometimes down.

At last, after Gila had held her three or four hours, one of the servants declared she would make her give her up, so she armed herself with a stick and went towards Gila. That cunning creature knew what was wanted as soon as she saw her coming, and quick as a flash she took Kit in one hand, and held her down to the ground behind her, while with the other she snatched up an old parasol to defend herself.

There was one member of the family against whom Gila had the greatest spite, and it is curious that all over the world monkeys have the same feelings. It was a parrot, which at first was placed on the same bar with the monkey. Whether jealous of her gay dress, envying her because she could talk, or whatever the cause, nothing so pleased Madame Gila as to play a trick on the unfortunate stranger.

The sly creature would begin by sitting quietly, and with the greatest seeming indifference, on her usual seat. Apparently she was deeply engaged in studying the state of things on the ground, carefully examining her own toes, arranging her glossy hair, even sometimes pretending to be asleep, or at least too sleepy to feel the slightest interest in any parrot. After keeping her eye on the enemy for some time Poll grew careless, plumed her gay feathers, and looked out sharply to see if anything to eat was approaching, for the monkey herself thought no more of dainties than did Poll. When she had almost forgotten the presence of her hereditary foe, Gila suddenly came to life. Quietly and slowly she stole up till within reach, when there came a quick grab, followed by shrieks of rage and pain. The parrot pulled herself away, generally with the loss of part of her gay tail-feathers, and moped and sulked for some time, while the monkey chattered with glee, exulted over her victory, and chewed the ends of the captured feathers.

But the laugh was not always on her side. Polly had a brain, and was not slow to plot revenge. She too could bide her time and steal quietly upon her victim, perhaps when she was intensely interested in lunch going on below, or taking a little nap in the afternoon. In her turn Polly crept across the bar, till near enough to give a tremendous peck at the soft flesh inside the end of her enemy's tail. Then the cries of distress came from the monkey, while the parrot chuckled with delight. This went on for some time, both of them refusing to be friends, and at last Polly was provided with a new residence.

One of the most troublesome things that the spider monkey did was to frighten children. The moment she saw one she gathered herself up, ready for fun, keeping perfectly still till the child came quite near, and then suddenly springing to her feet, flinging out her arms, with a loud growling cry like " O-o-o-o ! " It was a wild sound, and the youngster was sure to run and scream, which was the desired result, and greatly pleased Gila. But, strangely enough, there was one little girl, a mere baby, who was very fond of the monkey, and perhaps even more strange the fact that Gila was equally fond of her. The child's pet name was Chiquita, and she was a regular visitor at the house.

The moment she appeared, Gila opened her arms and welcomed her with a glad cry, and the baby, who could just walk, ran and threw herself into them with a warm embrace. After this, Gila sat down with her pet, and proceeded to look her over.

III.

THE MONKEY'S QUARTERS.

THE home of the Spider Monkey, as I said, was under the edge of the roof of the corridor. It was made thus: —

Two posts, some feet apart, were placed in the spot decided upon, and between them fastened a plank or bar, on which Gila could exercise as much as she liked. Over the bar slipped the ring at the end of her chain, which allowed her to stand on the ground, or to climb among the rafters under the roof. where a shelf was placed for a bed. On top of one of the posts was fastened a box for a seat or table, and her home was thought to be complete. So evidently did *not* Madam Gila; she wanted a swing of some sort, and she expressed her wishes by making one for herself, of the chain that held her. She would take hold of it with her tail to keep it loose so that it could not choke her, and then, throwing out arms and legs, swing to her heart's content. We took the hint thus given, and sent out to the Indians who make hammocks, so much used in that climate. and ordered one made of a suitable size for the monkey. When it was hung between her posts, there was never a creature so delighted. She had watched the family lying in hammocks in the corridor, and knew at once how to use it, and she could hardly be induced to leave it, night or day.

Monkeys differ as well as men. I have known those I would not have in the house, but my pet was naturally neat ; her ways from the first were almost civilized. Nothing annoyed her more than soiled or sticky fingers, and much as she liked syrup she often hesitated to take it, on account of the inevitable daubing. She did not use her long hair for a napkin either, but rubbed her hands against a post, or — sad to say — upon the dress of any lady who chanced to be near enough.

One of the most interesting sights was Gila in her morning bath. It was a shower from a watering-pot, and she sat perfectly still during the operation, rubbing herself all over, arms, back, and leg, like a well-trained child. Then she was brushed and combed, till dry and shining. But in spite of all her civilized ways, she could never be cured of a love of pranks. Her fingers fairly ached to be doing something, and her head, though small, held brains enough to be full of suggestions. No chance for mischief ever escaped her quick eye or was unimproved. If a woman came into the court to sell vegeta-

bles, which she carried on her head, Gila sprang
upon her, frightened her nearly out of her wits,
scattered her load far and wide, and scampered
up into the rafters where no one could reach her,
— grinning and chuckling over it till the excitement passed and she considered it safe to come
down. A special favorite with this monkey was
the woman who sold certain dainties made of
rice-flour and milk, which she carried in a tray
upon her head. Gila could throw herself out
very far from her bar by holding on with her feet,
and it was almost impossible for this woman to
get past her without giving the watchful creature a chance to snatch a handful of her wares.
As I always paid for them, possibly she did not
try to keep out of the monkey's reach.

When Gila got loose, as she sometimes did in
spite of our care, there seemed no end to the
things she would think of to do; and to think of
them was to do them, with her. If interrupted
in her fun, she would climb nimbly to the top
of a tall tree, and no coaxing would bring her
down.

One day she made much trouble by upsetting
and injuring many house-plants, and then retreated to her usual place. Every way was tried
to get her down, talking to her and tempting her
with fruit that she liked, but she would not
come. At last we thought of a certain jaguar

skin in the house. Monkeys have a deadly fear of this big cat, who is fond of them, — to eat, — and Gila had often been frightened by having this skin shaken at her, accompanied with growling.

A servant was told to bring it, but no sooner did Gila hear the order, whether she understood it or not, than she hastened quickly down the tree and sprang into my arms, where she always felt safe.

In the last chapter I spoke of the monkey "looking over" the baby she was fond of. This was a curious operation, to which Chiquita made no objection, though her mamma looked on with terror, for Gila was rough at best, and if angry she would bite in an instant. Biting, however, she did not think of. She gravely lifted the lids of the child's eyes, and peered under them with interest; satisfied with them, she investigated her ears, looking at them inside and out, before and behind, above and below, as earnestly as if she were a doctor searching for a disease. Then she gently lifted the little curling rings of hair, examining them curiously. Next she looked over her clothes, peering at hems, and trying to solve the mystery of ruffles, all the time as grave as a judge, with the air of wondering why the baby was white and not black; why her hair curled instead of lying straight like hers; why her clothes did n't fit close like her own; and, altogether, what was the difference between a baby and a monkey anyway. It was more than curious, it was almost sad. One could hardly help thinking that Gila was really making comparisons, and actually pondering causes in her mind.

The queer friends were extremely affectionate. Having allowed Gila to take the child in her arms, it was nearly impossible to get her out. Fortunately Chiquita liked it. If she had not been pleased and had objected, she might perhaps have been bitten, and her mother always dreaded it, for baby had a will of her own.

Coaxing never had any effect on Gila, and at any attempt to take the child she held on with arms and legs and tail, which gave her a great advantage over those who use arms alone. The only way they could be separated was by stratagem. Something would be done to attract Gila's attention, and Chiquita snatched away. This proceeding did not please either of them, and both screamed at the top of their voices.

IV

MONKEY MISCHIEF.

GILA was brimful of what is called the " mother instinct ; " she always wanted a baby to fondle. She was as fond of a doll as any girl, and played with a rag-doll I made her for hours at a time, though she generally ended by tearing its clothes off. But what can one expect of the most restless fingers in the world, — sixteen of them at that, — and obliged to pass away the long hours somehow? I never blamed her for tearing her doll. Unfortunately, she liked best a live baby. Not a cat, or any small animal, could come within reach of her long arms or her tail, but she would snatch it with either of the five that was nearest, and scramble to the top of her box, where she sat down to enjoy it, hugging it tight in her arms, no matter whether the head was up or down.

Among my pets was a baby tiger, as it is called in Central America, really an ocelot. This little fellow was very amusing, being as big as a cat, and as lumbering and playful as a kitten. Gila watched him with great interest as another live doll-baby, and if in a moment of frolic he chanced to get within reach, snap! she would snatch him and run to her perch. This insult from a monkey, who in a wild state is food for an ocelot, was not to be endured. The baby "yowled" in a fearful way, and scratched like any old cat. But Gila was not discouraged; she pressed him closer than ever to her breast, and played baby as long as she chose.

Poor Gila! she had trouble in finding a plaything to please her, but she did have one that was everything she could desire. Her only grief was that her pleasure did not last long. It was another monkey, one of a much smaller kind, a Friar monkey. She was almost too happy when he came, and she adopted him at once, hugging and kissing him, — at least if pressing her lips to him is kissing. Happily, he liked to be petted, and he enjoyed hanging on to Gila's neck, and riding around in her arms, as much as she enjoyed having him.

They were very happy for a while, but he was more mischievous than she, if possible, and his career was short. The first thing he did was to get loose, and, as I could not attend to him at the moment, I put him in my room, and unfortunately forgot him for some hours. The poor little fellow, left with nothing to do in a room full of wonders, naturally indulged his thirst for knowledge, and such a sight as greeted me when I opened my door I hope never to see again.

There was not a box or a bag, that he could open, but he had opened and thrown to the floor, and scattered everything. There was not a curtain in the room that he had not torn to shreds; not a picture that, in his search for spiders, he had not pulled down. The canopy over the bed he had destroyed; a glass of orangeade he had poured into the soap-dish; an inkstand he had upset, and made prints of an inky little paw all over my glass, where he had evidently been trying to get at the monkey he saw there. Lastly, when there was positively not another thing he could do, he had gone to sleep among the pillows, inky fingers and all. When I opened the door he sprang up in a panic, and was outside before I could catch him. He probably knew he should be whipped, for he ran to the roof and got away, and I never saw him again.

By this time I had become very fond of Gila, and she returned the affection, her greatest grief being that I would not let her sleep in my room, and be near me always, for she was a terrible coward and hated to be alone. When I opened the door in the morning, she stood up and greeted me with her most earnest " O-o-o-o." And when I bade her good-night, she screamed and chattered and begged so hard, that I could

hardly bear to leave her. A fright threw her
into an agony of terror, and one night I sprang
from my bed in terror myself, for I thought she
was being murdered. I fancied that nothing
less than a jaguar from the woods had hold of
her, from the noise she made.

The instant I opened my door she sprang
upon me, throwing her arms so tightly around
my neck I could scarcely breathe, much less get
away. I took her to my room and found that a
bat had bitten her and caused all this alarm. I
laughed at her, and tried to get her back into
her own quarters, but she made so great an ado
that I could not accomplish it, and that night she
passed in my room. A thunder-storm drove her
nearly wild, which is not so much to be wondered
at, for storms in that country are terrific. Even
the family gathered in one room, where Gila
always cried to accompany them, and I always
allowed her to do so.

She was a most sociable creature and much
company for me. I used to talk to her, and she
always responded and appeared to enjoy it. I
took pleasure in showing pictures to her, and
of this she was exceedingly fond. She would
pore over my photograph album, examine slowly
every picture, and look so wise that I could
hardly believe she had not her own opinions
about the faces it contained.

At one time I received a copy of a newspaper which had a good cut of a chimpanzee. I held it up to show her, curious to see if she would recognize it as a fellow-monkey. I was really startled to see how quickly she was affected. At first she merely glanced at it in a curious way, but in an instant she was greatly interested. She came down from the bar to examine it closely. After looking some time she actually put her hand behind it to grasp the creature, as I had seen her do to her own reflection in a mirror. It was plain to me that she recognized one of her kind.

When I had owned this monkey eighteen months, I prepared to go to my home in New England. Of course I could not think of leaving my pet, and I resolved to provide her with companions, lest she be too lonely. I collected five of her species, though one proved to be so homesick I had not the heart to take it from its friends. It moped and refused to eat, but watched the door from morning to night, looking earnestly at every one who entered, and so evidently longing for its friends that I feared it would die, so I sent it home.

V

THE MONKEY IN NEW ENGLAND.

WHEN I decided to take five spider monkeys to New England I had a travelling conveyance made in the shape of a large cage, of slats on all sides, so they would have air and light. Into this I put the four strangers. On first coming into close quarters, they had a general fight all round, but after this they made the best of it and lived peaceably together. Gila watched all this with interest, and not till the last moment did I put her in, too.

I had a feeling that it would not please her, and it did not. Her emotion was not anger, it was grief. She really seemed stunned, and too amazed for expression, that I could subject her to this indignity. This cut me to the heart. To see my dear Gila moping in a corner, refusing to eat, taking no part in the troubles or pleasures of the rest, made me feel very badly.

I coaxed and talked to her, but it was of no use, she would not be reconciled ; and when we reached the port where we had to wait for steamers, I took her out. But by this time she was really ill, — had chills and fever. I sent for a doctor and tried to make her swallow his prescription, but she got no better, and would eat nothing except a little she would sometimes take from my lips.

The voyage was a delightful thing for Gila. I kept her out of the cage, and she was the pet of the passengers. She was well supplied with dainties, and, above all, was never alone, — a thing she hated more than anything.

When we reached New York bay, no seasick traveller was ever more glad to see land than Gila. She was as interested as anybody to see the strange people and things. As we drew near the pier, I noticed that the people on shore laughed and pointed, and I found that Gila had climbed to a port-hole, and seated herself where her bright eager eyes could take in all the sights.

But now we must land, and now, alas! came the prison again. The noise and confusion had already driven the other monkeys nearly wild with fright; and when I opened the door to force my unwilling pet in, another got out. Gila clung to me, and between them a new bonnet I wore was torn to rags, as well as the hats of two men who were trying to help me. Finally all were secured, and, feeling that I looked as if I had been in a fight, and heartily wishing the troublesome monkeys were back in their native forest, I paid for the two hats, and started with my unmanageable freight for the quiet village in New England that was my destination.

The dismay of my family at my fellow-travelers, — for beside the monkeys I had several parrots and a baby ocelot, — the exclamations of surprise, not to say horror; the anxious " What can we do with five monkeys ! " "And a houseful of parrots! " "And a tiger ! " — all this I leave to the reader's imagination.

The first thing was to release them from prison ; so I took them out, one by one, and tied them in a row to the garden fence. A village with the usual number of small boys, five queer monkeys tied in a row, a free show ! The news spread like wildfire. The audience was perhaps not large, but it was all there was ; it was the whole population, at least the younger part.

A crowd surrounded the yard all day ; carriages drove up and stopped ; and every country wagon that passed within ten miles, I 'm sure, came around by our street to see the strangers. The monkeys enjoyed this succession of company ; nothing pleased them like an audience, and they cut all the pranks they could think of for the amusement of their guests.

At night they slept in the stable, where they huddled together under a quilt, and as it grew colder, I often had to go out in the night, roused by their cries, and give them more bedding.

Children did not usually come very near them, but one little girl, a neighbor, was very fond of them. She would play with them, feed them, take their hands for a promenade, and slap them, too, if they did not please her.

One morning we saw her come up behind them, take them one by one under the arms, and jump them up and down several times. They seemed to like it, too.

I soon found I did not enjoy keeping a menagerie, so I sent the four to the Philadelphia Zoölogical Gardens, where they all died one after another of consumption, as do nearly all the monkeys that come here. I sent also the ocelot, who had grown too big to be a pleasant pet in a house.

Of course I never thought of parting from Gila, and now I gave away most of my parrots, so as to devote myself wholly to her. But she did not revive as I hoped she would. She had never been the same monkey since the day she was put into a cage.

Now I hoped she would be well again, but I soon noticed that she was growing thin, and her appetite was most dainty. I sent for the choicest fruit, white grapes and everything I could think of to tempt her, but it was all of no use.

Before this she had ceased to go out of the house, and now she took to being wrapped in a shawl. She had the liberty of the house, and was only happy when lying in the sunshine, or held in some one's arms. She rapidly grew worse, and before long could not leave her pillow, on which she would lie close to the fire, insisting on having company.

She was not happy unless some one sat by her, on the last day, and put a hand on her or held her hand. This may sound like exaggeration, but every word is true. I never saw more " human nature " than poor Gila manifested in her last hours. If she could have spoken, her wishes would not have been more plain, nor her goodbyes better understood. And when she had turned her last loving glance on us, and gone gently to her last sweet sleep, you will not think it strange that a whole family shed tears over her body, and even buried her tenderly in the garden with flowers about her.

VI

GILA THE SECOND.

It is hard to take a monkey seriously. His business in life seems to be to amuse and entertain everybody who comes near him.

Whether he is so funny in his own native forests as he is when we get him with us, is not really known, but it is supposed that while young all monkeys are playful. Years and the responsibilities of life soon bring gravity to the most frivolous. To support life, and to preserve the same in the midst of enemies, is certainly a sobering process.

Taken from his wild life, tamed, protected and surrounded with comfort in his own climate, the monkey throws himself into his part with an enthusiasm and relish that leaves all other animals behind, and makes him the drollest, as he is generally the dearest, of pets.

We change all that, however, when we introduce him to a climate where he must always shiver. A monkey in our part of the world is no more like his brother in the tropics than a calm, fur-clad Eskimo is like his hot-headed, unclad fellow-man of latitude nothing.

It is a curious fact that, to the homesick
dweller among strangers, a human being with
foreign tongue seems not so near akin as an
animal, whose nature-language is as intelligible
in Patagonia as in Podunk.

My comforter and dearest friend in Nicaragua, said the same daughter of New England
who had owned Gila, was a spider monkey, and
the happiest hours of my banishment from home
were spent with an oddly assorted group of our
little brothers in fur, whose frolics amused, while
their fondness consoled me.

The scene of this true tale was the court and
surrounding corridor of a certain girls' school in
the city of Grenada, where pets were as plenty as
pickaninnies, and grave and gay alike delighted
in them.   Fancy an absorbed business man of
hurrying New York lavishing time and senti-
ment on a monkey or an armadillo, and conceive
— if you can — of a bustling Northern lady with
a tame jaguar at her heels, or a society maiden
bearing a tiny marmoset or squirrel - monkey
always on her shoulder.   In that city of the far
s>uth, these were daily sights which no one
thought of noticing.   Nor was it many weeks
after I began my work of teacher before my
affectionate scholars had, for my sake, peopled
the silent court with a motley family of beasts
and birds.

First in my heart was the spider monkey, one of the most loving of her emotional race, yet so prone to mischief that five minutes of freedom was as disastrous in the court as a cyclone. To find herself at liberty, was to fling herself with fatal instinct upon the choicest tree or plant. She wasted no precious seconds in deciding what to do, she simply did it, and two minutes was amply sufficient to strip a small tree of flowers or fruit and leaves, and turn to the next. Her ingenuity in planning, and her promptness in carrying out her plans, were truly marvelous. Yet how could I blame her? In sight of the tempting tropical growth, the restless creature spent long and tiresome days. With longing soul and itching fingers she gazed upon tree and shrub, plant and flower, doubtless planning a programme of operations should she ever achieve freedom. Success to the monkey was, however, embarrassment to the mistress; the principal looked annoyed, the gardener raged, and the cook openly scolded.

Quarters were arranged for her in the corridor, as they had been for her predecessor, and she was as quickly as possible placed in them.

After carefully studying out all the possibilities, she appeared perfectly contented with the plan, the familiar association with people making up to her for the restriction of her range.

The love and devotion of the monkey to his human friend is to me no less strange than it is touching. If gently treated, our four-handed brothers would live with us contentedly, and I believe could be trained to serve us as faithfully as the dog.

The heart's delight of my black-handed friend was a hammock, of proper size for her, which swung under the roof close to ours. More than half the long, quiet hours of the day were passed in that comfortable lounging place, one long, thin leg hanging out to keep her in motion; and so intelligent was she that, while everything else that her mischief-loving fingers touched was reduced to rags, the hammock never received the smallest injury. Strange to say, however, she never slept in it, and the monkey-fashion of sleeping is very different from that of man. She slept in a ball, sitting on her three-inch pole, held by a turn or two of her prehensile tail, her knees drawn up, and her face and nose buried in the fur between them. How she could breathe is a mystery, and why she did not fall off it is impossible to guess. The affectionate beast did not, to be sure, scorn a human bed, provided she could have a human bedfellow. Nothing pleased her better, in the hottest night, than snuggling up to somebody; and when — on rare occasions — she succeeded in freeing herself at

night, she whisked into the first bedroom she
came to, over the low slat-door common in that
hot climate, and in a few minutes somebody
awoke to find herself exceedingly uncomfortable,
with a very warm but very happy monkey beside her.

Excepting for her warmth, she was not an
unpleasant bedfellow, for she was as dainty in
person as the best-bred cat. It must never be
forgotten that a monkey, of her family at least,
is a different creature, when at home, from the
unfortunate menagerie beast with no means and
no heart for the niceties of the toilet. My pet
received a daily bath and brushing, that kept
her long, silky, golden-brown fur like a lady's
hair. She could never endure sticky or soiled
fingers, as we discovered to our cost when she
used our dresses as a napkin, and a bad odor is
so intolerable to her whole race, that it is com-
monly insisted upon that a monkey will die of
one.

VII

FROLICS IN THE CORRIDOR.

In the choice of friends my monkey was capricious, and beasts and birds enjoy friendships
and feel dislikes as well as man. The family in
the corridor at this time, besides the people, consisted of another spider monkey, of a disposition
so gentle that she was never confined, a baby
tiger (or ocelot), a tame deer, a squirrel, a kinkajou, several parrots, and a young dog. From
this queer party, all of whom were at liberty,
Madame Gila selected her friends and playmates,
the dog, and, strangely enough, the squirrel. Her
overtures were well received, and the three became intimate associates, enjoying daily frolics,
into which no other animal, however playful,
ever intruded.

Nothing could be more comical than the antics of this remarkable trio. The clever monkey
showed herself almost human in adapting her
ways to her playmates. She could play with the
dog in dog-fashion, with the squirrel in the
squirrel way, and then make the two submit to a
monkey frolic. How she reveled in those games!
They were her resource during the long school-

hours when her human neighbors were hard at their books and it was not time for dinner. If the dog — who was about half grown — made his appearance, she came out of her hammock like a flash, and pounced upon her friend, when the two rolled over and over on the floor, growling and snapping, pretending to be very savage, and no one could tell that it was not a big dog and a little dog at play.

Tiring of dog-play, she next insisted on his submitting to her sort of fun, which was to be swung by the tail or leg, to be held in her arms like a baby, and, above all, to be hugged. The dog endured honorably and with as good grace as he could for a while, but if it grew irksome he ran away, rejoicing doubtless that his too exacting friend could not follow.

When the squirrel joined in the romp, it assumed still another character and became a chase, after the custom of the nut-cracker tribes. Around and around went the three strange comrades in mad race, the squirrel leading, with long bounds, and tail undulating like waves behind him; the monkey galloping on all-fours, tail straight up in the air; and the dog running hither and thither, barking at the top of his voice. The affair always ended in a general clinch, and tangle of fur and legs and long tails, and barks and growls and chatters, so mixed up it looked as if they could never be straightened out.

But the heap speedily pulled itself apart, each of the three coming out with what belonged to him, and, though all had sharp teeth and knew how to use them, not a bite was given; nor did the two free ones run out of the monkey's reach, which proved that it was pure fun on all sides.

From the monkey point of view, the most valuable possession of the spider monkey was undoubtedly the long prehensile tail. Her bounds were well-defined, and not much mischief was possible, until the hot weather drove the family out of doors, and the corridors became breakfast and tea room as well as lounging place in general. After this change, came more or less opportunity for her to take a hand in affairs, and never was she known to miss her chance or shirk the responsibility.

Moved with pity for the solemn-faced, apparently drooping prisoner, some tender-hearted pet-lover would now and then unclasp the chain, and lead the sly rogue up and down the corridor for a walk. Meekness itself she appeared as she trotted along beside her friend, but under that indifferent exterior was a soul burning for action : every finger was alive, and that deceptive tail, swinging idly behind her, actually seemed to think and see for itself. Let it but

touch the corner of a table cloth, and instantly
there followed a crash of china, and the cover
and its contents lay on the floor. Should a
bottle fall into her clutches, the cork was drawn
with the dexterity of a professional butler, and
the contents, cologne or catsup, ink or ammo-
nia, scattered abroad over whatever and who-
ever it might concern.

A few catastrophes of this nature usually
hardened the most sentimental heart to her
coaxings, and after a while the table was established at a safe distance, books were no more
left on the chairs, nor pillows in the hammocks.
But one hope was left to agitate the captive's
heart, and that could not be removed. It was a
small window opening upon the corridor from
the room of the portress, Donna Louisa. By the
utmost stretch, the monkey could just lay hold
of the sill with one of her hinder hands and
cling, while the crafty long tail made an independent tour of inspection within.

The owner of the room had often been
warned, and was usually on her guard against
the artful enemy, but one day there arose in the
court a hue and cry that instantly brought the
whole family upon the scene. Here on the floor
was the portress, there on the roof the monkey;
on one side raving, shrieking, dancing about,
and cries, " O my Sunday gown ! " on the other

calmness, serenity, peace. If a monkey ever smiled in triumph at the happy result of long scheming, that rogue far out of reach on the roof did so, as she indulged in close examination of the precious finery fluttering in the morning breeze.

No one, except the raving owner of the treasure, could avoid laughing at the picture. But when the monkey began deliberately to tear her prize to pieces, the prank assumed a more serious aspect in the eyes of the monkey's mistress, whose purse would suffer for the fun. Commands were useless, coaxing unavailing, against such a pleasure; a ladder and a man were called in and the garment recovered, somewhat the worse for her handling.

These were pleasures that the monkey could enjoy while chained, but if by any chance she got loose, a wider field opened before her, of which she was quick to take advantage. There was the garden, a constant annoyance before her eyes, — so flourishing, so orderly, so plainly satisfactory to the gardener. How her fingers ‘ itched to take a hand in affairs out there! The instant she was free she rushed at it. She knew her time was short; she made the most of it. To destroy a full-grown banana plant took her perhaps ten minutes; to strip a small tree of leaves and twigs, not much longer; and five minutes was enough for her to pull plants and vegetables up by the roots, upset flower-pots, and turn order into chaos generally. Never was Gila the Second so happy as when engaged in this particular piece of work.

To dine, and to dine well, was the one important matter of the day with that dear four-handed torment. She ate what we did, had her individual tastes, and was as capricious and fussy as any chronic invalid who thinks of nothing but the next meal. The moment the table was spread in the corridor she decided what she would have, and have it she always did, no matter what it might be; for she brought her copious vocabulary of screams and cries to her aid, and made herself so very disagreeable, that no one could eat in peace till she was attended, and served as if she were the Great Mogul. She must have her coffee in the morning with us, and she insisted upon a part of every glass of lemon or orangeade drank in her presence.

However wearing the trials and annoyances of the day, we always forgave our poor little four-handed friend at night, for darkness brought her nothing but terrors. Never was beast so timid; a shadow — even her own — startled her, an unusual noise drove her wild, she screamed at a bat as if it were a tiger. The dark itself

appeared to fill her with horror; she crouched
and trembled and chattered; and a thunder-
storm seemed to her the end of all things. One
would think she had been brought up in a con-
vent, rather than in a forest full of sounds and
shadows.

VIII

BROTHER LONGLEGS.

No nickname was ever more aptly chosen than that given by the natives of Guatemala to the spider monkey, — Brother Longlegs. His limbs are the most conspicuous part of him. Somebody has said that he looks like four legs tied together in a knot in the middle, the knot, of course, being his small body. With his sprawling and grotesque motions, he is the delight of the menagerie, and the ease and rapidity with which he can travel the treetops of his native forest make him the despair of the ordinary hunter.

There is hardly a position possible to so large an animal that he does not sooner or later put himself into with the greatest ease. Sometimes, in their native woods, according to Humboldt, a cluster of spider monkeys may be seen, hanging by the legs, arms, and tails to each other, like some enormous overgrown and very lively fruit, swinging, chattering, and frolicking together, all suspended by the tail of one stout fellow who must have begun this queer sport.

The coaita, the best known of the family, is

an attractive-looking animal, clothed in rather long, coarse hair, of a glossy black color, with large eyes and a reddish flesh-colored face quite human in expression. He belongs to a branch named scientifically " Thumbless," because what should be thumbs on his hands are in fact merely stumps or single joints, although, to make up for this, he has very good thumbs on his feet, or hinder hands (which they really are). Perhaps the most useful member is neither foot nor hand, but tail. Not only is it strong enough to sustain the weight of a cluster of monkeys as mentioned above, but it is delicate enough to take birds' eggs out of a narrow opening. It is a help in walking, for the coaita is a tolerable walker, stepping carefully on the outside edge of his feet, never on the sole or palm, and steadying himself on his way by taking hold, with his tail, of every object within reach.

More than this, the tail is able to hold objects, and even to carry them off, and as a swing it cannot be equaled. So strong is its holding-on power that even after death it will firmly suspend the dead body for days. Nearly the whole length of the tail is covered with fur, like the rest of the body, but for several inches at the tip the under side is bare, and covered over with thick, black skin, which eminently fits it for its work. The old story of monkeys bridging a river, by hanging to each other in a long line, and swinging themselves back and forth until the lower one is able to grasp a tree on the other side, and thus forming a bridge for the rest to pass over, has been affirmed and denied till it is difficult to decide whether true or not; it certainly shows no more intelligence than many actions of the spider monkeys.

It may easily be seen, that to catch a coaita in his native forest is a hopeless task. With four hands and a tail to seize the branches and liana stems among which he lives, and with power to swing his light body five yards at each throw, as Dr. Oswald says, neither man or beast can follow him. The spider monkey, says the writer just quoted, " is nimble to a degree which makes one smile at the readiness with which that word is applied to such creatures as rats and raccoons." Nimble as he may be, however, strongly as his tail may hold, and many as are the devices by which this animal protects himself against his enemies, he cannot escape the worst of them, — man. The jaguar seeks his body to eat ; the large black and white eagle is said also to prey upon him ; but man has more wishes than merely to satisfy his hunger.

Not only is the unfortunate coaita possessed of savory meat upon his bones, but his skin is valuable, and, above all, he is in great demand

as a pet. The people of the countries in Central
and South America, where the spider monkey is
found, are the greatest pet-keepers in the world.
Not only monkeys of every sort, and interesting
small animals, share their homes and their affections, but every live creature, from a stupid-
looking tapir down to a mouse, may be found
living with people in the most amicable way.

The coaita is a favorite, partly because of his
droll performances and amusing antics, where-
ever he may live ; but much of his popularity
is the result of his gentle manners and amiable
disposition.   He is extremely affectionate and
social in his tastes ; being alone almost breaks
his heart ; and abusive or even unkind words
make him very unhappy, all of which has been
shown in the story of Gila.

Then, too, he is as fond of pets as the natives
themselves.   Other monkeys, even dogs or cats,
readily become the objects of his loving-kindness,
and have to endure hugs, not always agreeable
to them, which they sometimes resent violently.
Besides his gentleness, this creature is very intelligent and easily tamed, becoming so attached
to his owner that he will follow like a dog.   He
is not so restless as other monkeys of that country, but he is ingenious in his devices, and per-
severing in carrying out his plans.

One traveler tells of the interesting way in

which the spider monkeys managed to throw down upon his party large branches of trees, so many of them, indeed, that it was dangerous to pass beneath. A monkey first selected a dead branch in a convenient position, then, grasping with feet and tail a stout living branch near the former, he braced himself and pushed with his hands against the dead branch, using all his force, and generally succeeding in splitting it off, when it fell with a crash to the ground.

As to their perseverance, Waterton speaks of finding cases containing Brazil nuts, which are hard round objects somewhat larger than a croquet-ball and very hard to break, which the monkeys had worn smooth by the hands, in their efforts to break them open. They knew very well what was inside, for their fingers had been thrust through the small opening in the top, and their nails had picked and broken the corners of the nuts tightly packed away within. He knew it was the work of the monkeys, for he came upon them in the very act of pounding the cases on branches and on fallen tree-trunks, and one that he secured was dropped, in his haste to get away, by an unfortunate creature who had already spent many hours upon it. It was most curious, says the writer, to hear the pounding noise made by a party of spider-monkeys trying to break these hard cases.

VII.

THE OCELOT.

I. NICO.

WHILE the strange friendship between my spider monkey and her chosen companions was progressing, a curious attachment sprang up between a pair even more incongruous, natural enemies in fact. These were a deer not fully grown, and the baby-tiger or ocelot already mentioned.

This personage had come upon the scene at a very tender age, a few weeks it was supposed, and his entry was sensational. He was ferociously hungry; and though he did not know how to eat, he knew too well how to make himself heard. He cried and made such a disturbance that he was not welcome anywhere, till he fell into the hands of the spider monkey's mistress.

This lady, who had carried to that land of ease-loving people something more than grammar and arithmetic, namely, her New England "faculty," soon devised a way to feed the riotous infant, by soaking a sponge in milk, and then presenting it to his eager lips. He tasted, found it good, and settled at once to his meal, while his foster-mother had a chance to look at him.

A tiger " kitten " is a pretty little beast in gray and black fur, and he looked something like one of our familiar pussy's babies when five or six weeks old. But it was plain that this youngster lying so peacefully in her lap, and taking his milk from a sponge, was not intended to live in a house beside the fire and be coddled. His body was long and lank, for he must be able to run great distances in hunting, and to jump when he saw his prey ; his paws were enormous, for they must pull down and handle his meat for him ; his head was big and clumsy, and in every way he showed that he was born to live in the woods, to dine upon monkeys, and to catch them first.

But how his fate was changed when he went to a boarding school — a lady's pet. Food came to him without a hunt ; a warm bed was his for the taking ; anything he wanted he had only to demand, for the human race whom he feared and hated had become his servants. He was satisfied : he sheathed his claws once for all, and became a gentle, affectionate little beast, as tame — almost — as pussy herself.

I say almost, for he had one or two wild

notions that were not so easy to get over. One
was a fancy for something to suck, even after
he had teeth and could eat. It was strange,
but he never seemed to forget the comfort he
got out of that sponge in the first place; and
he quickly discovered that nothing was quite so
much to his taste as human flesh. So long as
one would allow him to hold finger or toe, or a
bit of arm or neck in his mouth, he was happy,
and would lie and purr like any old cat. But
he drew the flesh more and more into his mouth,
his sharp teeth were dangerously near; and no
one could help thinking that if he should happen
to break the skin and taste the blood he might
forget he was a tame tiger at a boarding school,
and suddenly show his wild side. So his friends
were a little nervous about indulging this taste
of his, and would not allow it.

Did he give it up? not he! Giving up is n't
the way to get anything, and the thought of
going without what he desired never came into
his head. He turned cunning; he watched his
chances. One lying in a hammock with arm
hanging out, or a school girl in the dormitory
with foot uncovered, became his victim. Whenever he found a sleeper, he stole quietly up to
her, and began a very gentle licking, so soft as
not to disturb the lightest sleeper. Gradually
he went further and got the toe or finger into

his mouth, and then he was in bliss, till his victim awoke and disturbed him, when he resisted, and growled and behaved like a naughty child. Of this trick he was never cured.

Another wild taste that made trouble in the household was the desire to have his food fresh and raw, and to select it himself. Half the fun of having something to eat was — in his eyes — the pleasure of hunting it. Not that he refused to be fed from the table; he had what our grandmothers used to call "a growing appetite," but when he wanted a little "sport" he knew how to get it.

One way was to waylay the cook. When that important person came in, with a pan on her head containing the meat for dinner, Master Nico, the tiger, knew that his chance had come. He was usually on the watch indeed, for he knew the hour the meat came as well as she did. As she entered, holding her head up, of course, he stole in behind her, and followed so closely and so lightly on his slippers of fur that she neither heard nor suspected him.

She passed into the kitchen and set down the pan, when like a flash the baby-tiger was upon it, teeth and claws every one buried in the piece of meat he had selected as he jumped. There he held on for dear life, for well he knew his claim would be disputed, and he braced himself for the storm. It came; shaking, scolding, and even beating did not stir him. He had to be actually torn away by main strength, but he carried part of the meat with him, and he had his excitement. The next day, or as soon as cook forgot to be on her guard, he repeated the performance, and never tired of it. Nor did he ever resent the rough treatment he received; he knew he was in mischief.

Another plan that he devised, to secure fresh fowl, was to look up the hens after they had gone to roost, kill one with a bite, suck its blood, and then leave it. One day the fowls were actually brought to his very nose, and though this tame way lacked the excitement of adventure, he did not refuse to accept.

A country woman came into the court to sell chickens, which she carried tied by the feet, and hanging from a pole across her shoulder, Nicaragua fashion. The cook proceeded to buy some, and buying anything in that land of leisure means talking half an hour over it. The ocelot meanwhile observed the defenseless chicks and also the absorbed traders. He crept up one side and seized one. The fowl remonstrated; the peddler shrieked, and demanded pay; and Nico slipped out of sight.

The cook, used to paying damages for the work of pets, agreed to the demand, but began

haggling about the price, when the wily tiger —
having been disturbed before he had finished —
returned stealthily, went to the other side, and
snatched another chicken. Upon this second
capture the cook hurried the vender out of the
court, and concluded her bargain in another
place.

TIGER TRICKS.

FOND as he was of fresh blood, the loyal beast never showed tooth or claw to his playmates on the corridor, the squirrel which he might have crushed with one blow, and the puppy almost as easily killed. On the contrary they had many fine frolics together. The squirrel ran over him, and played off his saucy squirrelish tricks on him, and Master Nico often laid his paw on the little fellow to hold him, but he never hurt him in the least.

To be fed on "scraps and leavings" was not at all to the taste of this savage baby. In the woods the tiger is king, and that it could be otherwise anywhere else never occurred to him. Intelligent as he was, he could never be taught to eat at the second table.

One day three lady teachers sat at dinner, one of them knife in hand, about to carve a particularly tempting roast chicken. Now Nico had marked that morsel for his own, and while the carver paused to make a remark, fork just ready to descend upon the fowl, there was a sudden bound, a snatch, a whisk of gray fur, and Nico and the chicken vanished together. Nor could they be found, though the premises were well searched. The chicken indeed was never seen again, though the tiger appeared after an hour or two, with an air of childlike innocence, not at all hungry, and quite ready to " kiss and make up."

Blood will tell, according to the old saying; and in spite of the fact that the days were all play and no work for the young ocelot, that he had always enough to eat, every comfort, and petting and spoiling to his heart's content, and that he had never known anything different in his life, he was never frolicsome like his domestic cousin the cat. He appeared always to look upon life as a very serious matter. He let the squirrel frisk about him ; he even seemed to like it, laid himself flat on his stomach and watched the pranks of his playmate with interest. Sometimes too he would lie on his back in his mistress' lap, and kick with his hind feet, like pussy ; though even then the wild taste showed in his trying to get his teeth down beside her finger-nails.

If not much given to frolic he seemed to have a kind of humor. He liked to hear girls scream, and servants scold, and to rouse the household generally. One way that he secured a pleasing hubbub was by knocking down the lamp chimneys. The girl who took care of the student lamps usually placed the chimneys together in a little grove, preparatory to cleaning them. This was an irresistible opportunity to Nico; the moment he saw them he walked in among them, swinging his tail, and knocking them right and left in fine confusion. The chimneys were imported, and costly, and many a hard-earned dollar his mistress paid for this mischief.

The only thing the baby tiger did that seemed like genuine play was in imitation of the ways of his own grown-up relations, for although he was brought up in a school — and a quiet girl's school at that — and had never seen wild ocelot life, he had a very clear notion of what it was like.

This little fun of his was a make-believe hunt, and his prey was a tame deer that liked to run and exercise himself by bounding around the edge of the court. Though his intentions toward his fellow-captive were most friendly, yet something in the movement evidently stirred his wild instincts. Creeping up one day cautiously, to a row of flower pots which the deer passed every time on its round, he crouched unseen, in true cat-fashion, and waited. As the "game" rushed by he gave one wild leap, and landed on its back, as neatly as though he had been taught by a savage mamma, instead of being the pupil of a gentle, peace-loving schoolmistress. The deer was startled, of course, but very quickly saw that it was only fun, and day after day the queer little play at wild life was reënacted, the deer seeming to enjoy it as well as his playfellow.

The story of the little tiger is like the story of all wild pets. At first they are very interesting, and the people about them, in trying to make them contented and happy, really become slaves to them. As they grow older they expect the same treatment. A tiger held in the lap when he is the size of a cat will expect the same when he is as big as a calf.

The happy life in the corridor, like everything else that is pleasant, — and no less everything unpleasant, which we sometimes forget — came at last to an end. The ocelot grew exacting as well as cunning with age, until in his twelfth month his demands became so troublesome that it was resolved, in solemn family conclave, to put him out in the country to board till the approaching vacation, when he should accompany his doting mistress to New England. That land, however, he was destined never to shock with his own lawless manners and customs, for in a moment of playfulness he tried the hunting trick on a big dog. The beast did not like it, he resented the liberty, and the baby tiger paid for his joke with his life.

The monkey, too, the merry, happy-hearted queen of the corridor, became ill before she left her native country, and her mistress had neither the pleasure nor the pain of taking her pet to her New England home.

VIII.

MONKEY BABIES.

I. THE COITA AND THE ORANG-UTAN.

THE grown-up coaita is not hard to tame, but the baby is never anything else than tame. Of course a youngster cannot be caught except on the death or severe injury of its mother, for it is never alone an instant, always riding on her back, and holding on from the first with four hands that never let go. A baby coaita of a month old is a lank, ungainly creature with long black hair. When by the death of its mother it falls into the hands of men, it does not fail, at least among the natives, to get most tender care, even sometimes to the extent of sharing the native baby's natural food, it is said.

Its great want at this age is warmth, and I heard of one owned in our part of the world which was kept alive through a cold winter by being bagged, literally, every night with a pair of fluffy puppies. A large bag half full of straw and wool was the bed *in* which, not *on* which, the three strange bedfellows passed the night. Their owner opened the bag, dropped puppies and monkey together into the bedding, then closed the mouth of the sack and tied it, to make sure that no one escaped. Throwing the curious bag-load into a barrel, he covered that up closely as well.

They did not smother, they throve and grew fat on it, which proves, I am sure, that fresh air, or even any air, is quite unnecessary to babies of the monkey and dog families.

The monkey baby is very much like a human youngster; but sooner than our little folk he learns to go alone and care for himself, and by the end of two years, it is said all the funniness is out of a monkey. Rev. Samuel Lockwood tells the story of one who lost his fun all in a moment, and from being full of tricks and very happy, became a sad, joyless creature, because of his lost faith in man. It happened in this way. He lived in a shop of basket-makers, and among other tricks was expert at catching sticks that men threw to him. When this ceased to be a novelty, and the workmen were tired of playing with him, they took to teasing, and the cruel thing they did was to throw a hot poker to him. He caught it, but it ended his fun for life.

The voice of the coaita is soft and musical, with those he is fond of, when in confinement, and louder, with a wailing or mournful quality, when calling to his fellows in freedom. He also utters a sort of barking grunt, and doubtless indulges in many other cries that are not reported.

One would never look among the monkeys for a solemn baby, yet the little Orang-Utan is said to be as sober as his mamma herself. Never do the hunters, or the natives of Borneo, where this baby lives, see troops of youngsters at play together in the woods, as they do of other young monkeys, but each young orang stays quietly with his mother till he is able to care for himself. Then he goes with the whole troop through the trees, where their days are spent, eating fruit, young leaves, buds, and tender shoots, and drinking the water found in the leaves, — unless it happens to be dry weather, when they have to come down to a stream.

This baby does n't like to come to the ground, and he is as awkward there as men are upon trees, hobbling along in a clumsy way. But when he gets among the branches he is at home, walking along on them nearly straight up, though going on all fours, because his arms are so much longer than his legs that he need not bend over to use them.

Thus the orang goes on till he comes to the end of the branch, when he reaches a limb of the next tree, swings himself over, and walks on. He is said never to jump about from branch to branch, as do some monkeys, but always to hang on to one till he gets hold of another; which proves him to be a very prudent fellow, I am sure.

Like other monkeys, this little creature has no special home; and when night comes, and he gets sleepy, his mother makes a bed for him with her. She does it by breaking off branches and laying them crosswise on other branches of the tree. In a very few minutes she will make as nice a bed as any monkey baby could desire.

The bed is made low down in the tree, and if it rains, the natives say a big leaf is used as a cover. Should one of the poor fellows be wounded by men who want his skin, he hurries to the top of the thickest tree he can find, and makes himself a bed in which to die, or to lie and get well if he can. He chooses his place so well, and makes it so thick, that he cannot be seen from below.

The baby orang has often been brought to our menageries, and we know him well as a captive. He is amiable enough when well treated and indulged in his whims. Like a human baby, he likes to be " coddled " and kept warm, held in laps and nursed tenderly. Like them also, he does n't like to sleep alone, nor to wake up and find his nurse gone; and he is quite able to make his likes and dislikes known, for he cries and screams and roars, amazingly like a human baby.

He has his notions, too, about his food; some things he likes and others he does not. He will quickly push from his mouth the morsel not to his taste, and, if another is given, scream and kick like any two-handed infant.

Like all little people he is fond of toys, and, in fact, he must have something to amuse him, or he will roll on the floor, with all four hands grasping at the air till he catches something — no matter what, — when he holds on for dear life. The thing he likes best to seize is hair, and unfortunate is the man who lets him get his fingers into his beard. Every finger is bent over at the last joint so that it makes a perfect hook, and, once clutched into a thick beard, it is almost impossible to get them out; especially as he is very strong, being able to break nearly any cage or undo almost any chain.

In one thing, however, he is not in the least like our dear little human babies; he does n't look like them. His face is wrinkled like a very old man's, and his eyes look wistful and careworn. When sick he weeps, actually sheds tears, and moans; and when angry he pouts — a pout that no girl or boy, however cross, can equal. He makes his mouth almost into a trumpet.

Though solemn, this baby is not stupid; he readily learns to live on our food, and to eat and drink in our way, using a spoon as well as a cup for tea and coffee. A naturalist, who was spending some time in Borneo, caught a baby orang-utan a foot long, and kept it alive three months. It acted very much like a young human baby, cut two teeth, and was learning to walk, when it died, because he could not get proper food for it.

In color the orang-utan is a reddish chestnut, and his name is *Simia Satyrus.*

II

OTHER MONKEY BABIES.

THE baby gorilla is a strange little creature, with jet-black face and hands, and a gray coat. He is not pretty to look at, — according to our notions, — with his big mouth, flat nose, and head sunk in his shoulders ; but he is very interesting. This is partly because we haven't known much about him till lately, and partly because he belongs to the largest and strongest of the monkey race.

Of course this baby is of the greatest interest to his mother, who pets him, caresses him, and takes the best of care of him, letting him ride on her back till he is old enough to look out for himself. He never has a nursery, and his mother's back or arms form his only cradle. With her he sleeps in the trees, anywhere they happen to be when night comes on.

As soon as he is big enough he eats fruit and leaves, and runs about on the ground on all-fours. He looks very odd running about, for he turns his foot over and treads upon the side, and doubles his hands to tread on the knuckles, where the skin grows thick and hard.

The truth is, he is most at home in the trees, and one of his favorite amusements as a youngster, at home, is to swing on the branches, leap or fling himself from one tree to another, in games with his playmates, all shouting and screaming like so many playful girls and boys.

He is full of life and fun, and has gay times till he grows up and looks on the serious side of life. Then he becomes strong and fierce and savage, — at least toward men. He can hardly be blamed for that, however, for the men he knows are either hunters trying to kill him, or keepers forcing him to live in a cage, which of course he hates, as does everybody with any spirit.

There's only one way that men can catch this baby, and that is by shooting his mother. When she falls he falls with her, for the first thing he learns in the world is to hold on well; for, of course, as she travels about in the trees she uses her hands as well as her feet, and he must cling for himself. He does, and not until his mother is dead can he be secured, and then when he is taken away he cries and screams like a baby.

If the young gorilla is kindly treated he is gentle and affectionate, very fond of play, and as pleased to be petted as any human baby, as well as dainty and neat in his manners. He will sit on one's knee and lean against his breast, and become so much attached to a kind keeper as to pine away and die if he leaves him.

Then, too, he is very fond of a frolic, clapping his hands, thrusting out his tongue, romping about a room, swinging and leaping, and galloping around on knuckles and feet, very much like one of our own little folk. He is very good to mind what he is told — when he understands — and quick to learn what is wanted. The thing he likes best to play with is a gentleman's long beard, and that you know our babies like, too.

One of these little fellows that was brought from Africa — his native land — was cross so long as he was shut up, but after he reached the ship to go to England he was let out, and then became as good-tempered and amiable as anybody, played with the sailors, romped and frolicked to his heart's content. His special favorite was a dog, a bull terrier, who was not very good-natured, but happened to like the gorilla baby, and they were great playfellows.

One writer who knows a good deal about gorillas has said that even in babyhood this animal is always ill-tempered and savage. No doubt all that he knew were so, for every one he had was either chained up, shut in a cage, or wore a split stick over his neck ; probably, too, they were beaten by servants. This is enough to make anybody cross, especially a little wild baby frightened out of his wits at being stared at.

One baby that this writer told about was perhaps two years old, and so strong it took four men to hold him. When he broke loose from his cage, no one dared go into the room to catch him, he was so savage. They opened the door carefully and threw a net over him, and when he was well tangled in it, they rushed in and shut him up, in spite of his kicks and struggles. If any one came near this very naughty baby, he rushed at his visitor with yells, tried to seize him, and acted as if he would tear him to pieces.

The gorilla baby is an anthropomorphous (or man-shaped) ape, and his name is *Troglodytes Gorilla.*

III.

THE DROLLEST BABY.

Baboons are almost the ugliest of the monkeys to look at. They have dog-shaped heads, with eyes deep-set and close together, and their faces have ridges and swellings and queer colors, so that they are really hideous, to our notions.

But, in spite of their looks they are most interesting animals, because they are so fond of each other, and so amiable and full of fun in babyhood. Dreadful-looking old fellows, that look as if they could easily eat up a baby, are extremely fond of the little ones, and as tender and careful as any human nurse.

Some droll stories are told of baboon babies in menageries. In one place there were two mothers with infants, and the others of the tribe, when allowed to go in the cage occupied as a nursery, gathered about the mothers, put their arms fondly around them, and begged by their actions to hold the baby a little. The mothers allowed them to do so, and the little ones were passed around among the visitors, each one holding a baby a few minutes carefully, and then passing it on. At last, after every one had taken the child, it was given back to its mamma. Such a performance among animals is very extraordinary.

Another one that was in a menagerie in Paris was in a cage alone with its mamma, and when about eight days old papa was allowed to go in to make a call. He embraced mamma and the baby, and then sat down by her and took the little one in his arms. Pretty soon the rest of the baboon family were introduced to the interesting cage, to call on the infant, which they had been wild to do.

Each one wanted to take it, of course, but this mother was not so obliging, or so trusting, perhaps. She would not let any one touch it, and if urged she gave the teaser a slap. They all sat around her and moved their lips as though talking.

The baboon baby has probably a better time out of a menagerie. He sleeps in a den in the rocks, rides on his mother's back, and eats berries and fruit and roots, besides insects. Nothing is funnier than to see a party of these wild youngsters at play. They are specially fond of sliding down hill. They select a nice, grassy place, and down they go, sliding and rolling over and over like great balls of fur, chattering and carrying on like a party of children. They run about on all-fours on the ground, and if in a hurry they gallop, but they are not often seen on trees.

The little baboon is a jolly fellow, always full of pranks and jokes, such as slyly pulling the tail of some dignified old fellow. But this performance turns out not so funny if he gets caught, for a pinch or a bite is the pay he gets. Like other little folk, the baboon baby sometimes loses his temper, and the ways he takes to show his anger and to threaten the enemy are very strange. He opens his mouth wide as if yawning, or he pounds his fist on the ground as a naughty child will do.

As they grow old, like many other animals, and especially monkeys, they grow more savage and cross, and of course are not so interesting. But they are very cunning. They go in large parties together, and often visit the crops of the farmer. When they do this they keep watchers on the lookout, and, though usually quite noisy fellows, they are as quiet as any other thieves who know they are taking what does not belong to them. If an unlucky baby chances to make a noise he gets a smart slap, and naturally he soon learns to keep still when on an excursion of that sort. This fellow lives in Africa, and his name is *Cynocephalus Hamadryas.*

IV

THE MOST AMIABLE BABY.

THE most amiable and altogether lovely monkey baby that ever lived among people is the baby chimpanzee. He is a roly-poly little fellow, with a large head and long arms, and his face looks like one of our babies', for it is light-colored and smooth, and the hair on his head is longer than it is in most monkeys.

For two or three weeks, too, he is as helpless as a human baby, and has to be carried everywhere; but then there begins to be a difference. He tries to get about alone, and it is only a few weeks before he can run around as well as any of his family. He goes on all-fours, stepping on the knuckles of his hands, and never laying them out flat on the palm.

He grows up faster than our babies; at six weeks old he begins to eat fruit, and long before a human baby leaves off his milk diet, the baby chimpanzee eats everything his mother does, and is able to scramble about in the trees in a way that no human baby, however old or skillful, can ever do. He is quite grown up at nine or ten years old.

This baby is very fond of a frolic, like other little folk. In their native woods in Africa groups of young chimpanzees are sometimes seen playing together like a party of children, running after each other, turning somersets, swinging, shouting and screaming, and, above all, drumming on a log with a stick, which they like to do as well as boys like to play on a regular drum. When they are hungry they eat fruit or plants. It is as a captive that the little chimpanzee is best known, and here he behaves curiously like a child. For one thing, he doesn't like to be shut up in a cage, and he does like to sit on the lap of his nurse and be "cuddled" like a baby. He will put his arms around her neck and cry, when she puts him down. In fact he sometimes makes a great fuss about it, screams, and throws himself on the floor, and kicks and rolls over. But this is not often. Generally he is gentle and affectionate and full of play, laughing when he is tickled, and giving little grunts of pleasure, while his hazel eyes twinkle with fun.

The most interesting thing about the young chimpanzee is his desire to do as people do. He greatly likes to get hold of clothes to wear. He easily learns to eat with a spoon and fork, to drink from a cup and saucer, and to enjoy our food, even hot tea. When he grows older he even goes so far as to like to smoke, and to shake hands.

He is very cunning and full of curiosity, as well as intelligent. He can thread a needle, and lock and unlock doors or boxes, using a key as well as anybody. Also, he likes to tease. One in the London Zoölogical Garden had great fun in jumping upon a cage where lived some marmosets. These little creatures chattered and crouched in a corner, and were frightened half out of their wits. This much pleased Master Chimpanzee, and in a few minutes, when they had got over their fright, he would pounce on them again. When denied what he wanted, this little fellow pouted and made harsh barking sounds, but if very angry — as I said — he screamed and rolled on the floor, opening his mouth wide, and throwing his arms around to hit everything he could reach. He was very affectionate to other chimpanzees, putting his arms around them, and he had great romps with an orang-utan.

All monkeys — as well as children — are fond of playthings, and the one I am telling about was presented with a doll. He hardly knew at first whether to be afraid of it or not, and it was tied to the end of a rope. Then he could swing it and jerk it, which he did with great glee, laughing to see the antics of the thing. His laugh is not so hearty as ours, but a sort of loud-whispered " Ha ! ha ! "

There has been a notion among people that a monkey cannot smile, much less laugh, but that has been proved a mistake. Close observers, as Darwin and Buckland, affirm that the chimpanzee can do both.

The baby chimpanzee likes to play with children, and whatever they do he does after them. If the youngsters make up faces at him, he returns the compliment, thrusting out his lips till they look like a trumpet. Like the children, too, he is fond of sweets and milk ; and, unlike them, he will wash his own hands and face. He's a droll little fellow, with high shoulders, and big ears, and beautiful white teeth, and his name is *Troglodytes Niger.*

MONKEYS WHO WORK.

BEFORE I end this account of monkeys, I want to say a little about some who have been taught to work.

Monkeys are very much like people in their ways. Whether the fact pleases us or not, we are obliged to admit it.

The baby monkey — droll little bundle of fur that it is — acts wonderfully like the darlings of our nurseries. It puts its fingers in its mouth, and it creeps on the ground; it plays with toys, and it laughs when tickled; it weeps when grieved, and it screams when angry; it moans when ill, coos when caressed, and squalls when left alone, — exactly as do human little folk.

When it is a little older it plays and quarrels, drums on hollow logs to make a noise, jumps, swings, and performs feats of strength, so like those in which our own youngsters delight as to be amazing to one who sees them.

Yet they are "full of mischief," we always say; and people chain them up or shut them in cages, where they fret themselves nearly wild. It is pitiful to see the restless creatures with nothing to help pass away the tedious hours; and it is not necessary that it should be so.

Should pet monkeys, then, be allowed to smash the vases, scrub the wax-dolls, choke the baby, and perform the thousand other pranks their four busy hands ache to do?

No, indeed! There's a better way. They can be cured of mischief, just as two-handed little people are, — by giving them something to do; by teaching them to work.

This is not so hard a task as one might think. Monkeys that live with people are always imitating what they see done, and work is as easy to learn as mischief, — if one only thinks so. Why, then, should they not be taught to work? Long ago in Egypt it was discovered that four hands can be more useful than two, when properly trained. In those far-off days our four-handed relative was employed in certain services about the gardens. He it was, instead of a clumsy man-servant, who was sent into the trees to gather figs and other fruits. He handed them down to his master below, as we learn from the old sculptures; though, to be sure, the picture-story does not fail to add that he did not entirely forget himself, and that many a tempting morsel found its way into his mouth. Would a boy have done any better?

This useful Egyptian servant belonged to the

baboons, or dog-headed monkeys ; and although when young the baboons are good-tempered enough and easily taught, their experience of life makes them cross, so that an old baboon is one of the ugliest of animals.

Monkeys in our own days do such wonders, that perhaps we have no reason to doubt the story, told by an old writer, of one which used to be sent regularly to buy wine. This animal was a coaita, one of the spider monkeys, which are able to walk upright without much trouble. When sent on his errand, he had the jug in one hand and the money in the other, and he was wise enough to keep the money till the wine was ready, when he would pay for it and carry it home.

Nothing is harder work than playing for the amusement of other people ; and more than two hundred years ago monkeys were taken to England, to perform there in shows. They were dressed in fine clothes, in the fashion of the day, and they behaved with perfect propriety. They saluted the guests and one another by taking off their hats and bowing politely ; they danced together the stately minuet and other fashionable dances, and they imitated many other social ceremonies.

They also did other things more difficult, if not quite so dignified. They performed on the tight-rope, and turned somersets with lighted candles or baskets of eggs in their hands, without putting out a light or spilling an egg. An old English writer, Evelyn, who kept a diary, tells about a visit he paid to these learned animals.

In our day the monkey has not escaped from work, — in fact he is learning to do more every day; and the time may perhaps come when he will be a common worker. In one part of Africa he is taught many useful tasks about a house, — such as holding the torches, which are used there to light up the room for a feast. Several monkeys are placed on a bench, each with his light to hold. There they must sit, and see others eat and drink and have merry times, while they dare not stir hand or foot lest they put out the lights. If they are very good, when the feast is over they have a supper themselves. But sometimes one gets tired and impatient, and flings his torch among the guests, and that monkey gets something else instead of his supper.

One of the most teachable of the race is the chimpanzee. In their native land young chimpanzees are caught when mere babies, and are taught to be very useful. They are able to carry pitchers of water on their heads as the people do, and to keep a fire going, or to watch the cooking. When they live among white people, they learn to sweep and dust, to clean boots and brush clothes.

Should they go to sea, they still contrive to be useful at furling sails and hauling ropes with the sailors ; and if their home is with carpenters, they become equally expert with tools, even using hammer and nails properly.

Monkeys are quick to learn politeness and refined manners, for nothing seems to please them so much as to copy the ways of those about them. It is easy to teach them to eat with knife and fork, to drink from a cup or glass, and to use a napkin ; they like it, too, and soon relish our food, and show likes and dislikes as strong as the most notional " spoiled child " in America.

They take kindly to other ways of ours, — they enjoy sleeping in beds, and soon learn to " make them up." They like to be warmly dressed, and can readily learn to dress themselves ; and they have their own tastes in colors.

In the Island of Sumatra the common monkey is the bruh, or pig-tailed monkey, and he becomes a docile and intelligent servant. What he has to do is to gather cocoanuts. Of course nothing is easier for a four-handed fellow than to climb the tall trees and throw down nuts ; but the bruh does better than that; he selects the nuts, gathering none but the ripe ones; and, what is more, he picks only as many as his master wishes.

So useful is this animal that gathering nuts has become, one may say, his trade, in that part of the world. A man, having captured and trained a gang of them, marches them around the country to get in the harvest, hiring them out on different plantations. Then, when the nuts are all picked, or the laborers too numerous, gangs of them are taken to the English colonies at Cape Town, and hired out like any workmen, or coolies, as they are called.

A Siamese ape has reached a step higher, it is said. The story is told by an Austrian who lived in Siam that this ape is able to tell by the taste whether coin is good or bad, and merchants employ him for the purpose of detecting counterfeits.

Within a few months a gentleman of India has tried his hand at training monkeys, and he reports to the Asiatic Society of Bengal his success in teaching them to pull punkahs. A punkah — perhaps you know — is an immense fan, hung from the ceiling, and moved back and forth by means of a rope outside the room. It keeps a whole room cool, and in that climate is necessary to enable a white man to eat or sleep with any comfort. A monkey who can pull one, then, is as useful as a man, and is a true worker.

Another valuable monkey is the chacma of Africa. When young, this baboon is very teachable, and is often kept by the Kaffirs as a domestic animal. He takes the place of a dog, growling when a stranger comes near; and if it becomes necessary to defend his master's property, he is much stronger than any dog.

The chacma easily learns to blow the bellows of a smith, and to drive horses or oxen; but his greatest use in that country is to find water.

In the hot season, when the earth is parched and springs and streams are dry, the owner of a tame chacma takes him out to hunt for the water they all must have.

The intelligent monkey seems to know what is wanted, or perhaps he knows by his own feelings what to look for, and he goes carefully over the ground, looking earnestly at every tuft of grass and eagerly sniffing the breeze on every side. Whether he scents it or not is not known, but if there is water in the neighborhood he is sure to find it. It may be a deep spring, in which case he sets to work digging down to it; and it may be a certain very juicy root, which often serves instead of water. He gets that out also: and let us hope he has his full share of it, to pay for his work.

Like the rest of the monkey family, the chacma gets very ugly as he grows older. An English gentleman who spent some time among the Kaffirs tells of an old chacma which liked to play jokes, rushing at the women as they went by, seizing them by the ankles, and acting as fiercely as if he were about to eat them up.

The thing he liked best, however, was a little animal — a young dog, for instance — to pet and "play baby" with. He would hug it and dandle it, as a girl does a doll, till the puppy made too much resistance, and then he would seize one leg or the tail, swing his pet around once or twice, and fling it far away.

The latest report of a monkey that works comes from Florida. It is a chimpanzee, trained to wait at table ; and its owner says it does the work of four negro waiters. It wears a livery, and carries a napkin in a proper way. Its only weakness is so irresistible a fondness for sweets that it is obliged to take toll as it serves them.

INDEX.

OUT-DOOR BOOKS

Selected from the Publications of

Houghton, Mifflin and Company,

4 Park St., Boston; 11 East 17th St., New York.

───◆───

Adirondack Stories. By P. DEMING. 18mo, 75 cents.

A-Hunting of the Deer; How I Killed a Bear; Lost in the Woods; Camping Out; A Wilderness Romance; What Some People call Pleasure. By CHARLES DUDLEY WARNER. 16mo, paper covers, 15 cents, *net.*

The American Horsewoman. By ELIZABETH KARR. Illustrated. New Edition. 16mo, $1.25.

At the North of Bearcamp Water. Chronicles of a Stroller in New England from July to December. By FRANK BOLLES. 16mo, $1.25.

Autumn: From the Journal of Thoreau. Edited by H. G. O. BLAKE. Crown 8vo, gilt top, $1.50.

A Week on the Concord and Merrimack Rivers. By HENRY D. THOREAU. Crown 8vo, gilt top, $1.50.

Birds and Bees. By JOHN BURROUGHS. With an Introduction by MARY E. BURT, of Chicago. 16mo, paper covers, 15 cents, *net.*

Birds and Poets, with Other Papers. By JOHN BURROUGHS. 16mo, gilt top, $1.25.

Birds in the Bush. By BRADFORD TORREY. 16mo, $1.25.

Birds through an Opera-Glass. By FLORENCE A. MERRIAM. In Riverside Library for Young People. 16mo, 75 cents.

Bird-Ways. By OLIVE THORNE MILLER. 16mo, $1.25.

Cape Cod. By HENRY D. THOREAU. Crown 8vo, gilt top, $1.50.

Country By-Ways. By SARAH ORNE JEWETT. 18mo, gilt top, $1.25.

Drift-Weed. Poems. By CELIA THAXTER. 18mo, full gilt, $1.50.

Early Spring in Massachusetts. Selections from the Journals of HENRY D. THOREAU. Crown 8vo, gilt top, $1.50.

Excursions in Field and Forest. By HENRY D. THOREAU. Crown 8vo, gilt top, $1.50.

The Foot-Path Way. By BRADFORD TORREY. 16mo, gilt top, $1.25.

Fresh Fields. English Sketches. By JOHN BURROUGHS. 16mo, gilt top, $1.25.

The Gypsies. By CHARLES G. LELAND. With Sketches of the English, Welsh, Russian, and Austrian Romany; and papers on the Gypsy Language. Crown 8vo, $2.00.

Homestead Highways. By H. M. SYLVESTER. 12mo, gilt top, $1.50.

In Nesting Time. By OLIVE THORNE MILLER. 16mo, $1.25.

In the Wilderness. Adirondack Essays. By CHARLES DUDLEY WARNER. New Edition, enlarged. 18mo, $1.00.

Land of the Lingering Snow. Chronicles of a Stroller in New England from January to June. By FRANK BOLLES. 16mo, $1.25.

Little Brothers of the Air. By OLIVE THORNE MILLER. 16mo, $1.25.

Locusts and Wild Honey. By JOHN BURROUGHS. 16mo, gilt top, $1.25.

The Maine Woods. By HENRY D. THOREAU. Crown 8vo, gilt top, $1.50.

My Garden Acquaintance and a Moosehead Journal. By JAMES RUSSELL LOWELL. Illustrated. 32mo, 75 cents. *School Edition*, 40 cents, *net.*

My Summer in a Garden. By CHARLES DUDLEY WARNER. 16mo, $1.00.

Nantucket Scraps. Being the Experiences of an Off-Islander, in Season and out of Season. By JANE G. AUSTIN. 16mo, $1.50.

Nature. "Little Classics," Vol. XVI. 18mo, $1.00.

Nature, together with Love, Friendship, Domestic Life, Success, Greatness, and Immortality. By R. W. EMERSON. 32mo, 75 cents ; *School Edition*, 40 cents, *net*.

On Horseback. A Tour in Virginia, North Carolina, and Tennessee. With Notes on Travel in Mexico and California. By CHARLES DUDLEY WARNER. 16mo, $1.25.

Pepacton. By JOHN BURROUGHS. 16mo, gilt top, $1.25.

Photography, Indoors and Out. By ALEXANDER BLACK. With Illustrations. 16mo, $1.25.

Poems. By CELIA THAXTER. 18mo, full gilt, $1.50.

Poetic Interpretation of Nature. By Principal J. C. SHAIRP. 16mo, gilt top, $1.25.

Prose Pastorals. By HERBERT M. SYLVESTER. 12mo, gilt top, $1.50.

A Rambler's Lease. By BRADFORD TORREY. 16mo, $1.25.

The Rescue of an Old Place. By MARY CAROLINE ROBBINS. 16mo, $1.25.

The Round Year. By EDITH M. THOMAS. Prose Papers. 16mo, gilt top, $1.25.

Rural Hours. Charming descriptions of scenes about Cooperstown, N. Y., where Cooper's novels were written. By SUSAN FENIMORE COOPER. New Edition, abridged. 16mo, $1.25.

The Saunterer. By CHARLES G. WHITING. Essay on Nature. 16mo, $1.25.

Seaside Studies in Natural History. By ALEXANER AGASSIZ and ELIZABETH C. AGASSIZ. Illustrated. 8vo $3.00.

www.ingramcontent.com/pod-product-compliance
Lightning Source LLC
Chambersburg PA
CBHW030111030726
47498CB00007B/2339